Gentle surf fingered its way up the sand to bubble and lap across their legs.

Leaning over her, Grace was breathing hard. "Do you want me?" she demanded huskily.

Trapped in the intensity of her gaze, Dawn struggled to find the words. "I don't know what to do," she whispered.

Grace's arms closed around her. "Yes you do."

And she was lifted into the air, Grace's mouth on hers, warm and intoxicating. Moments later she was lying on something soft. Her towel. Grace was caressing her, long sensual strokes which extended from her breasts to the parting of her thighs. Unbearable heat spread through her pelvis. Parting her legs, she placed her hands on Grace's shoulders. "I want you," she said.

Grace moved over her, blotting out the moon, erasing the pulse of the ocean, the green jungle smell, until Dawn could feel only her, smell only her. She shivered as Grace slid an arm beneath her hips, trailed warm kisses across her stomach and over her thighs . . .

Saving
Grace

Jennifer Fulton

The Naiad Press, Inc.
1993

Printed in the United States of America on acid-free paper
First Edition

Edited by Christine Cassidy
Cover design by Pat Tong and Bonnie Liss
    (Phoenix Graphics)
Typeset by Sandi Stancil

Library of Congress Cataloging-in-Publication Data

Fulton, Jennifer, 1958–
    Saving grace / by Jennifer Fulton.
        p.   cm.
    ISBN 1-56280-051-5 : $9.95
    1. Lesbians—Fiction.   I. Title.
PS3556.U524S28   1993
813'.54—dc20   92-43360
                                                              CIP

For my daughter Sophie
May she grow up in a clean Pacific

Acknowledgments

My long-suffering family knows how much I depend on their unqualified support. I am also indebted to Christine Cassidy and Katherine V. Forrest for their editorial guidance. To Greenpeace and the many environmental activists in this region, I give my thanks for their courage and persistence. The day has not dawned on which I can look at the beauty around me and take it for granted.

About the Author

Jennifer Fulton is a full-time writer living in Wellington, New Zealand. She is the author of *Passion Bay* and *Saving Grace,* and under the pen name Rose Beecham, is responsible for *Introducing Amanda Valentine.* Although writing is Jennifer's chosen vice, she is also devoted to fly-fishing, opera, and fine cooking.

CHAPTER ONE

It was a typical Sydney summer's day. The sun burned tyrannous and hot, and in the harbour milled pleasure craft with such cliched names as Pussy Galore or Freudian Slip, their decks plastered with basking socialites and hunky dark-haired waiters. Trailing raucously in their wakes, gulls squabbled over the occasional jettisoned olive or stunned fish.

The Sydney Opera House, target of a throng of camera-happy tourists, loomed against a postcard sky. On the Manly Ferry locals yawned over cans of

Foster's and a whimsical breeze toyed with the long soft hair of a brace of truant schoolgirls.

Rearranging her own blonde ponytail, Dawn Beaumont glumly surveyed the scene. "I'm bored," she declared.

"Is that all?" Her cousin Trish studied her with a hint of exasperation.

"Isn't it enough?"

Trish heaved a sigh and dug about in her handbag, producing a handful of tissues.

Dawn pushed them away. "Oh, what do you care! It's not your life." Tears had slithered beneath her sunglasses.

"Of course I care, Dawn." Trish offered the tissues again and waited while Dawn mopped her face. "I know it's frustrating, but injuries like yours don't heal overnight."

"Frustrating! That's the understatement of the year. It's driving me 'round the bend living at home. Mom keeps on stuffing me full of food and Dad won't shut up about me swimming in a goddamned disabled team, and there's all the trophies . . ." Dawn blew her nose fiercely. "They won't put them away. I've asked."

"Give them time, Dawn. They need to come to terms with it too."

"You make it sound like I'm dead. I bloody deserve to be . . ." Dawn gazed at the water churning over the ferry's bow. Ordinarily she loved the trip across the harbor: the air so clean and salty, the hum of the city drifting discordantly across the water. But these days nothing gave her pleasure. She might as well be dead, she thought bitterly. Her life was ruined.

"Dawn." Trish's voice held a hint of rebuke. "We've already had this conversation. It's been six months since the accident." She glanced at Dawn's legs then looked quickly away. "You've got to stop blaming yourself."

"It *was* my fault."

"We all make mistakes. I think you've paid for yours."

"Well, some people wouldn't agree!" Since the accident she'd heard it a million times. *You were so lucky. It was a miracle.* And somewhere lurking behind the forced brightness, that unspeakable question: *How come you survived and Lynda was killed?* By rights it should have been the other way around. Lynda was younger, an even better medal prospect for the Olympic squad. And she was sweet, gentle and kind — everything Dawn wasn't.

Tears plopped off Dawn's chin onto her hands. "They all think it should have been me. They —"

"Now hold on," Trish interrupted. "That's simply not true and you know it! Everyone wants you back on your feet —" She broke off, her pained expression revealing annoyance at the insensitive choice of words.

"Well don't hold your breath!" Dawn kicked the walking stick propped beside her. "Just look at me, leaning on this bloody thing like a granny. I'll never swim again. My life is over ..." She choked back a sob. Trish was probably sick of the sound of her by now. All she ever seemed to do was cry and moan.

But Trish took her hand. "You need some time out, Dawn, time away from all of this. From your parents and the reporters and everything. You need to get away from Sydney, go someplace where you can think. Take my word for it," she insisted as Dawn began a protest. "A change is as good as a rest. Besides, it's time you started planning your future.

"I don't have a future."

"Nonsense!" Trish gently shook Dawn's shoulders. "You're only twenty-two. Of course you have a future. You won't be swimming in the Olympics, but neither will most of the population, and I think we'll survive."

"You don't understand," Dawn said sullenly.

Trish ignored her. "It's decided then. I'm going to book a holiday for you, miles away from here. I know the perfect place."

"No. Absolutely not." Dawn had a bad feeling about this. Somehow over the years, she had fallen into the habit of doing exactly what Trish wanted. It was because Trish substituted as a big sister, she supposed.

Already Trish was acting as if she'd agreed to everything. "You're going to love it," she promised.

"Trish, I said no." It might have been easier to sound resolute if the idea of getting out of Sydney wasn't so appealing.

"But you meant yes," Trish said smugly. "Darling, it's written all over your sad little face. Why fight it?"

"I suppose you're talking about that rotten island," Dawn grumbled.

Trish was wreathed in smiles. "Well, you had such a ball last time . . ."

* * * * *

4

Grace opened her eyes and waited, frozen between the sheets, for a sound to rise from her throat. What should have been a scream was just a sigh, escaping from her lips like air from a soda bottle. With a concentrated effort, she moved first her hands, then her feet. Then she waited. For what, she wasn't certain.

The Dream. With shaking fingers, she touched her face. Her skin was clammy. She examined her hand carefully. In the wan first light, it was pale and unsullied. It dropped to her chest and nestled there.

Grace stared around the hotel room. Bland, uncluttered walls stared back. A full-length mirror gaped on the opposite wall. Abandoning her bed, she drifted toward the tall copper-haired woman reflected there. Dark, shadowed eyes met hers, the pupils huge. For a moment, something flickered in them, the shock of some horror freshly witnessed, then there was only blankness. Grace turned away, gathered up some clothes and retreated to the impersonal solitude of her bathroom.

A few hours later, she was in the bar sipping a margarita and listening absently as the band mutilated a Springsteen song. She hated drinking alone in hotels, evading the wishful eyes of men on the prowl. Worse still, she hated competing with them for women to chat up. She wished she had been able to fly straight out of L.A. yesterday when she'd arrived. But Robert B. Hausmann himself had insisted on seeing her before she left for the Cook Islands.

Drumming her fingers, she drained her glass and signaled for another drink. It wasn't like the CEO of Argus Chemco to be late. She wondered how far her boss had got with the Moon Island deal. In Grace's experience, Hausmann played to win, but this time she suspected he might have to walk away from his pet project.

It wasn't that easy to find an island suitable for chemical dumping. There were so many factors to consider: location, proximity to habitation, strategic and/or political importance. And these days, even with the financial incentives companies like Argus could offer, most poorer nations were growing reluctant to permit foreign dumping on their shores.

Argus had been hunting for an appropriate site in the South Pacific for over a year now, staving off clients with material to dump who were offering highly lucrative contracts to Argus to solve their problem. This time, however, Hausmann seemed convinced they would succeed. Already the Cook Islands' Premier had indicated an interest in the Argus proposal. And who could blame the guy — responsible for some flimsy banana republic economy that was totally dependent on foreign currency earnings.

Grace idly stirred her drink, then tensed as someone spoke her name.

"Dr. Ramsay?"

Turning, she faced a woman somewhere in her thirties, black wavy hair to her shoulders, fine olive skin and a body to die for. Smiling a slow invitation, she said, "You're speaking to her, and it's Grace, by the way."

The delicious stranger shook her hand briefly. "I'm Camille Marquez, Robert Hausmann's assistant."

"Delighted to meet you." Indicating a chair, Grace wondered what had happened to Hilda Gruber, Hausmann's usual defender. "Can I get you a drink?" she offered, enjoying the way Camille's skirt tightened across her thighs when she sat.

"Martini, thanks." Camille delved into her briefcase, extracting an envelope that she passed to Grace. "Mr. Hausmann asked me to apologize on his behalf. He was called back East on an urgent matter. These are the latest briefing papers for the Moon Island Project."

Grace tore open the envelope and scanned the contents. The purchase of Moon Island seemed highly likely, but negotiations were, of course, sensitive at this stage. Grace's assessment of the island was to be carried out with the utmost discretion and she was to confirm as soon as possible the suitability of the site and the likely scope and time frame of the necessary site preparation. Hausmann was presently in negotiations with an important new client — the sooner he knew the probable date for the commencement of dumping activities, the better.

"When is Mr. Hausmann leaving for Rarotonga?" Grace inquired.

Camille consulted her Filofax. "He has a meeting arranged with the owner of Moon Island in four days."

That would give her a chance to make a quick preliminary evaluation of the site. "Tell him I should be able to confirm viability by then," she told Camille.

"I'll let him know." Camille was busily penning. "Is there anything else I can assist you with?"

Grace met her eyes and smiled languidly. "Do you have any plans for this evening?"

CHAPTER TWO

"Well here we are." Trish humped Dawn's bags onto the check-in scales. "You okay?"

"Of course I am," Dawn said peevishly. She wished people wouldn't keep on asking her that. They only did it out of guilt because they were relieved it was she and not them.

Scanning the faces around her, she caught strangers looking hurriedly away. When you were young and limped along on a walking stick it changed everything. People either stared or pretended you weren't there. You couldn't go to a bloody barbecue without some fool wanting to put a blanket on you. In summer, for God's sake.

Even now Trish was interrogating the ticketing clerk. Where would she be sitting in relation to the bathroom? No she couldn't stagger all that way up and down the aisles. What if it was a bumpy flight? Dawn prodded her, said it didn't matter, but Trish shoved a boarding pass into her hand with the pointed comment that cripples are people too.

"Maybe I shouldn't go," Dawn said miserably as they waited for her boarding call.

Trish laughed. "I can see you're determined to have a lousy time."

"I am not!"

"Then cheer up, angel. And don't worry about your parents. I'll handle them."

Dawn cringed. Her parents had no idea about this expedition. They thought she was going away for a long weekend to the Blue Mountains. She could hardly bear to contemplate their reactions when they found out. Since the accident, it was all they could do to let her use the bathroom by herself.

Trish patted her hand. "If it makes you feel any better, at least they won't be able to contact you out there."

Dawn's jaw dropped. She'd forgotten how primitive Moon Island was. "You mean they still haven't got proper phones?"

"Just the famed crank-handle party lines," Trish said cheerfully. "Great, isn't it? Peace and quiet guaranteed."

* * * * *

10

That wasn't exactly balm to her troubled spirits, Dawn reflected nine hours later as she hovered outside what passed for Rarotonga International Airport. She was hot and tired and the announcement had just come over the pager that the connecting flight to Moon Island was running late. That was typical, she thought, slouching grumpily against her luggage. And it was probably the same wreck of a plane as last time, too. Perhaps it had crashed en route.

Ineffectually licking at her dry lips, she dragged her sun hat farther down her face. She was a fool to have come back here. She should never have allowed Trish to talk her into it. After the last time you would have thought she'd learned her lesson. What a disaster that had been. Normally she would never have holidayed in a place like the Cook Islands. Her idea of a perfect destination was Queensland, where everyone ignored the beach and swam in hotel pools so they didn't get sand in their pants.

But back then Trish had already booked and paid for the vacation to Moon Island, only to find she had to cancel at the last minute when she landed some big photography contract at Ayres Rock. She'd offered Dawn her tickets and it had sounded great. A tropical island, luxury villas, golden beaches.... The sneaky bitch hadn't said anything about the place being run by weirdos who only let women stay there.

It had been two weeks of relentless boredom. No phones, no electricity, no night life and no men. And to top it all off, a hurricane hit the island and everyone had to spend two terrifying nights in the next best thing to the Batcave with some smart-ass Kiwi playing the Girl Wonder.

Cody Stanton. The mere thought of her made something crawl in the pit of Dawn's stomach. She could still picture the wretched woman loping along the jungle paths with that own-the-world walk. Who did she think she was, anyway?

Unzipping her cabin bag, Dawn rummaged crossly for her painkillers. Her legs were aching. Perfectly normal, the surgeon had said when he removed the plates and screws: an unstable comminuted fracture of the tibia and fibula, femoral fractures in both legs. What did she expect?

Dawn pushed the subject away. She didn't want to think about her ugly, useless legs. She just wanted to get to her destination and lie down. Where the hell were these people anyway? Didn't they want visitors? Fuming, she hobbled indoors and bought herself a can of Coke. She snapped the tab viciously, dropped some Panadol and guzzled the contents. Then she returned to her luggage and sank down, waiting for the pain to subside.

To her frustration, Cody Stanton's face hovered persistently in the foreground of her mind, dragging Dawn back to her last day on Moon Island three years before. After the hurricane a group of guests had been at Villa Luna, the main house, waiting to be rescued by the cargo boat. Dawn had gone for a walk on Passion Bay, only to find Cody there too, with Annabel Worth, the woman who owned the island. They were in each other's arms, kissing exactly like lovers.

Dawn had taken one mortified look and fled. Cody Stanton was a lesbian, she'd realized stupidly.

For some reason the knowledge still made her knot up inside.

"Dawn?" A voice made her jump guiltily. "Is that you?"

A pair of long, neatly muscled legs stood before her. Dawn followed them up past slim hips, an ancient Levi's shirt and a wide mouth, into a pair of candid gray eyes. Cody hadn't changed a bit. "Of course it's me," she snapped. "I've been dying out here wondering when you'd bother to turn up."

Cody grinned, no sign of remorse. "It's good to see you. Are these all yours?" She nudged Dawn's luggage with her toe.

Jerking a brief nod, Dawn snatched up her stick and wobbled to her feet. Chin jutting, she dared Cody to make something of it.

But the taller woman was already striding off across the tarmac. "Follow me," she said over her shoulder. "It's not far."

Dawn glared. What a bitch. She might have had the decency to shorten her stride or check if her guest was okay. But no, she barely seemed to have noticed Dawn's predicament.

By the time they reached a small tatty-looking silver plane, Dawn was puffing with exertion and resentment. Firing a suspicious glance toward the hangar, she demanded, "Where's your pilot?" Surely they weren't going to roast out here for the next few hours waiting for some patch-up job. Dawn knew all about that kind of thing from her last visit.

"Bevan's on holiday," Cody replied blandly. "Annabel's flying the shuttle."

"Terrific," Dawn sniffed, watching Cody stow the bags. Amateurs.

Finishing her task, Cody waved to someone. Turning automatically, Dawn faced a stunning blonde woman who looked as if she'd just walked off the pages of *Vogue*. Annabel Worth, the owner of Moon Island . . . the woman Cody lived with.

"Dawn." Annabel removed her sunglasses and smiled warmly. "I'm so glad you've come back."

Mumbling a hello, Dawn tried not to be startled by Annabel's porcelain pale skin and her strange, pinky-lavender eyes. You got used to it when you saw her everyday, but it was a bit of a shock after all this time.

"Let's get out of this heat," Annabel said. Tossing her sun hat into the rickety plane, she pulled a decrepit leather flying jacket over her silk shirt and helped Dawn aboard. "The Dominie's going like a rocket," she commented, as if Dawn were interested. "We bought a Rapide for spare parts last year and Bevan's in England now, shopping for a couple of new motors for us."

Dawn shuddered. "I don't know why you don't just buy a whole new plane, instead of trying to keep this old wreck in the air."

Next to her, Cody was frowning. Dawn instantly regretted her comment. Annabel was obviously soppy over the stupid plane and maybe they couldn't afford a better one. She hadn't meant to be tactless, but she was fed up, and even as she sagged back into her hard little seat, a stabbing queasiness rolled through her gut. The painkillers. She'd taken them on an empty stomach. The warm Coke probably hadn't helped either.

As Annabel started the plane, she stuck her fingers in her ears, wishing she could block out the desperate whine of the engines, the foul petrol fumes and the jarring vibration. It would also be nice if Cody Stanton wasn't sitting so close she was virtually in her lap. Dawn twisted to check the seats behind her. They were jammed with supplies.

The plane lurched. Bracing herself, she closed her eyes. If they were going to end up in the drink, she didn't want to watch. Several teeth-rattling minutes later, one of her hands was pulled away from her ear and Cody's voice said, "It's safe to look now."

Trying not to jump at the contact, Dawn bestowed a dirty look on Cody then turned to gaze pointedly out her window. They were airborne and the motor noise had tapered off to a bearable thrum. She couldn't help but marvel at how blue it all was below. But for the hint of whitecaps, the ocean seemed inseparable from the sky. There was no sign of land on the vast, curved horizon. The sun sat high above, gleaming off the Dominie's silver wings, and the plane felt very small and vulnerable as it nosed its way farther and farther from civilization.

Despite herself, Dawn began to relax. It felt quite exhilarating to be flying away, to be on her own. Three whole weeks on a tropical island. A house to herself, nobody fussing around her, needing her gratitude. When you were sick it was lonely and crowded all at once. But she had escaped!

She felt like laughing out loud, but instead she frowned at her own elation. It was the drugs, of course. They tended to distort her judgment. In the hospital she'd had morphine, and as far as Dawn was concerned the drip never flowed fast enough. Once she was off morphine there came Voltarin and the refined cruelty of slow release. To compensate, you had to take Panadol or Digesic every few hours, and Dawn had quickly became a slave to the pill trolley.

These days, she mixed her own cocktails. You had to be careful. Voltarin was stomach-ulcer territory. One a day was the limit. More than that and you spat blood. Sometimes she didn't care and popped an extra anyway. But mostly she got by on Panadol top-ups. Lately she'd promised herself she would cut back, stretch out the hours between doses. But she didn't have the willpower. When you had constant pain, all you could think about was stopping it.

Cody and Annabel were talking. Dawn caught snatches — Bevan had done Shuttleworth, some big plane museum . . . . Annabel's mother was coming to stay. Her mother! What did she think of Annabel and Cody? Dawn felt sorry for the poor woman.

She shifted in her seat, weariness overtaking her again. The petrol fumes were giving her a headache and the vibration grinding along her legs reminded her that her pills were only thinly disguising the reality of her pain. She should have stayed home, she told herself once more. She should have pulled herself together and got on with the business of life. After all, she was one of the lucky ones. She could have had her spine destroyed, become a paraplegic. What right did she have to feel sorry for herself?

Tears stung. Dawn wiped them on her knuckles. Then she stared at her hands. They had been quite pretty before the accident, fine-boned and soft-skinned. Now they were covered in scars. Gingerly she touched the tender new skin, and looked up straight into Cody Stanton's searching eyes.

"Are you all right?" Cody asked softly.

If anyone asked her that again, she'd scream. Why couldn't people just mind their own business? "Of course I'm all right," she retorted.

For a moment Cody held her gaze, then with a small defeated shrug she turned away.

"Passion Bay to your right, folks," Annabel announced.

Dawn told herself she couldn't give a damn. But she peered down anyway, taking in the white beach, the dense green of the jungle, the unmistakable shape of Villa Luna with its courtyard garden laid out like a brightly patterned handkerchief in the center.

"I hope you know how to land this bloody crate," she grumbled as they dropped toward the treetops.

Annabel swooped low over the landing strip then suddenly, jarringly, she wound on full throttle and they shot straight back up into the clouds, climbing giddily while Dawn squealed ineffectual protests from the back seat. Seconds later the world turned upside down and the tiny plane seemed to fall out of the sky.

"What the hell do you think you're doing!" Dawn shrieked.

Annabel didn't answer until they had landed and the motors were finally silenced. Then she turned to Dawn and said in her polished drawl, "I thought I'd see if this bloody crate could manage a roll or two, before we made our crash landing." Her eyes were cool and unsympathetic. "If you're planning to throw

17

up, would you mind doing it outside. I'd hate to ruin my outfit cleaning up after you."

"You were a bit hard on her, sweetheart," Cody said later that evening. "I mean, she's obviously had a terrible accident."

Annabel glanced up from a folder she was leafing through. "Am I hearing this correctly? Are you really defending the dreadful Dawn?"

"She's not that bad," Cody objected. "She's just immature."

"You said that last time she was here, Cody. And that was nearly three years ago. When will the excuses run out? When she's retired, maybe? Or does walking with a stick exonerate one from common good manners?"

"You could have got us all killed."

"When have I ever done that?" Annabel smiled sweetly.

Cody tossed a cushion at her. "I've died a thousand deaths in that plane, and you know it. Anyway, it wasn't such a bad idea of Dawn's."

"What idea?"

"Buying a new plane. After all, the Dominie's fifty years old. Can't we just put it in a museum and get a Lear or something?"

"Maybe we could, if we wanted to accept this." Annabel tossed the folder she had been holding across to Cody. "Read it and weep."

Cody admired the leather binding. "What is it?"

"It's five million dollars, darling. Someone wants to buy Moon Island."

Cody's brow furrowed as she thumbed through the pages of legalese. "But who . . ."

"Argus Chemco," Annabel supplied. "They're a big chemicals multinational. I'm meeting Robert Hausmann, their CEO, in Avarua later this week to discuss the offer. Evidently Argus are planning to expand their South Pacific operations and they want to establish a base in the Cook Islands."

"But Moon Island is miles from anywhere. It seems like a lot of money to pay for an office no one can find. Why don't they just buy New Zealand?"

Annabel smiled lightly. "Maybe that's next. I phoned Hausmann and told him he's wasting his time."

"Well." Cody tossed the portfolio aside. "That's the end of the Lear then."

"I'm afraid so, sweetheart." Annabel reached for Cody. "We'll simply have to resign ourselves to being stuck out here in the tropics, slumming it on white beaches and getting cheap thrills at the expense of brats like Dawn Beaumont."

Burrowing into her, Cody slid a knee between her thighs. "Sounds like hell," she murmured.

CHAPTER THREE

"So you're not dead after all." The voice came from the same direction as a stream of irreverent morning light. Camille Marquez was sitting at a small breakfast table calmly squeezing lemon into two cups of tea. She was immaculate in raw silk pants, butter yellow shirt, thick gold bracelets.

Her head splitting, Grace elbowed herself upright, taking in the clothing strewn across the floor, the used smell of the bed linen, Camille's latex dams clinging to the bedspread. Her teeth felt furry and, rubbing her eyes, she caught the unmistakable scent of woman on her hands.

"Oh my God," she groaned. "We ..."

"I'm afraid so." Camille crossed the room, handing Grace a cup of tea. "You weren't bad."

"Well thanks." Grace choked on her first sip, images flitting across her mind — Camille laughing, the two of them sliding hot and naked amidst a tangle of sheets.

"You might have performed better if you weren't drunk," the other woman added.

Grace deposited her cup and saucer on the bedside table and tenderly massaged her temples. Evidently she'd made the Big Impression. "I'm not usually such a slob," she said, wondering if she'd fallen asleep or something.

"And I'm not usually such a bitch." Camille indicated a neatly folded pile on the dressing table. "I got some fresh clothes for you. Take a shower, and we can get breakfast before you catch your plane." She checked her watch. "I'm going out now to send some faxes. I'll be about fifteen minutes."

Time management. The woman was obviously a formidable exponent of it. You had to be, Grace supposed, if you were organizing someone else's life as well as your own. Easing her legs off the bed, she forced herself woozily to her feet.

Camille was sorting papers into files. Glancing at Grace, she remarked, "Great body. Are you always so free with it?"

Grace frowned. Was she being called a slut now? "Only with kindred spirits," she returned tightly.

That earned a laugh. "You think I sleep with just

anyone?" Camille snapped shut her leather briefcase. "I felt like good sex and I thought you might be able to deliver."

"Well, I'm flattered." Grace was at a loss for words. Apparently Camille orchestrated her sex life as methodically as her work.

Right now she was looking Grace up and down like a used-car salesman contemplating a trade-in. "You fuck around a lot, don't you, Grace?" she said. "Is that why you avoid having orgasms? You like to stay detached?"

Heat seeped into Grace's cheeks, and before she could prevent herself, she'd folded her arms defensively across her body. "I enjoy myself," she said. "Sex doesn't have to be orgasm-centric, surely?"

"Sure." Camille shrugged, collected her briefcase and started toward the door. "So if it doesn't matter, how come you take care of yourself afterwards, eh?"

The door clicked resolutely behind her and Grace flopped back onto the bed. "Well fuck you too, Camille," she muttered.

Several days later Annabel Worth strolled into the cool of the hotel lobby. She was right on time. When you got a note from the Cook Islands Premier insisting you meet some big shot on "a matter of importance to the Cook Islands," you turned up. She'd even dressed for the occasion, wearing the kind of outfit she might have power-lunched in back home in Boston a thousand light-years ago. But here on Rarotonga a pink silk Chanel suit was guaranteed to fetch a few boggling stares from locals who seldom saw the owner of Moon Island in anything but cotton shorts and a straw hat.

Removing her sunglasses, Annabel checked her French plait and crossed the parquet tiles to the bar. A man rose as she approached. He was sandy-haired, considerably shorter than she and somewhere in his late forties. Like her, he was formally dressed, his suit and tie making no concession to the tropical surroundings.

"Ms. Worth?" At Annabel's brief nod, he extended his hand. "Robert B. Hausmann. Pleased to meet you."

Ushering her into a chair, he signaled a waiter. With slight puzzlement, Annabel observed him as he ordered their drinks. Robert B. Hausmann? The name seemed familiar. No doubt she had encountered it somewhere in the financial circles she'd once occupied.

"You're from back East, Mr. Hausmann?" she opened politely.

"New York." Annabel wondered about his accent. Highly educated, but rough edges. "Bronx and proud of it." He had confirmed her suspicions. "And you? Boston?" This was said with the self-satisfaction of a man who knew he was right on the button.

Nodding, Annabel contained a smile. She recognized Hausmann's type — a short man with something to prove.

"Beautiful city, Boston," he remarked expansively. "Nearly lived there once." His tone suggested Boston's loss was greater than his. "Have you settled in these parts now, Ms. Worth?"

"I spend most of my time here. Although I do keep an apartment back home."

This caught his interest. "You have family in Boston?"

"That's right."

His eyes narrowed. Then, with a snap of the fingers, he declared, "Theo Worth. You're his daughter?"

Annabel tensed slightly. "You know my father?"

The response was enthusiastic. Robert B. Hausmann had evidently golfed with her father. He waxed lyrical over her parent's game, then asked her about the greens on Rarotonga.

"I'm afraid I wouldn't know. I've never shared my father's passion for golf."

Her companion waved an apologetic hand. "Then I bore you, I'm sorry." Leaning back in his chair, he surveyed her with a calculating expression. "So, what are your passions, Ms. Worth?" He flashed a set of perfectly even teeth and Annabel wondered whether she'd taken an instant dislike to him because he reminded her of a politician or because he wore a little too much expensive aftershave.

Their drinks arrived and she sipped her mineral water, then said coolly, "I'm sure we're not here to talk about our passions, Mr. Hausmann."

"No indeed." His glance slid past her breasts as if by accident. "I'll come straight to the point. As you know, we want this deal."

He expanded briskly. Argus Chemco was planning a major expansion of its Pacific Basin operations. This meant new offices around the region, employment growth, and millions of dollars in foreign currency earnings. It was very exciting . . . he was personally *very excited.*

The Pacific Basin was a growth marketplace for Argus. The next decade would be a boom time as Southeast Asia threw off the shackles of Third World poverty and embraced the consumerism that had made America great.

Annabel stemmed his flow. "So what exactly does Moon Island have to do with this vision, Mr. Hausmann?"

"I'll be frank, Annabel . . . . may I call you Annabel?" He treated her to another brochure-perfect smile, confiding, "I have a feeling we're going to get to know each other very well." He had the good sense not to pat her knee, but Annabel guessed it was a close thing. "You've read the offer. Is there anything else I can tell you?"

As Annabel shook her head, he produced another leather-bound portfolio from his briefcase and extended it to her. "Excellent. This is the sale contract. As you will see, I have already signed."

Annabel placed the folder beside her unopened. She had finally caught on to his identity. Robert B. Hausmann had surfaced during the corporate raids and leveraged buyouts of the eighties. Considered something of a wonder boy, he had touted his CEO skills around the business underbelly of New York, selling himself to the highest bidder, then generally orchestrating a takeover by some shark who would offer him an even bigger package.

Argus had done just that, absorbing, under his initiation, the rival company he headed, only to find that he promptly deposed their own Chief Executive in a coup that had scandalized Wall Street. But under Hausmann, Argus had flourished, swallowing competitors, scaling the Fortune 500 list and paying out unprecedented returns on its stock. So who was complaining?

Robert B. Hausmann embodied everything Annabel detested most about the world she'd left behind. He was spawned by, and now promulgated, a value system that routinely destroyed viable companies, chopping up their assets and selling out their employees for the sake of fat fees for a greedy few at the top.

"It's a very generous offer," he summarized in a self-congratulatory tone. "I think you'll agree that the combination of cash and stock is most advantageous. I'm sure I don't need to emphasize the growth we are anticipating in the medium term. Suffice to say, the offer is worth five million dollars at today's values, but considerably more in the future if you hold the stock." He paused, perhaps to add weight to his words. "We both know that in some ways private wealth is a secondary consideration here, Annabel. I'm talking about the economy of these islands . . ."

The gall of the man, Annabel thought. He had read her like a book. The Cook Islands were desperate for foreign investment. The locals needed jobs and the government needed the tax. Annabel cared about that and he knew it.

"I've spoken at length with the Premier and he has assured me of his personal commitment to the project." Hausmann drove home his advantage. "I know you'll feel the same way when you consider what this could mean to the Cook Islands people."

Big finish. Soft-spoken Hausmann was a real carpetbagger.

"I appreciate your concern, Mr. Hausmann,"

Annabel said more calmly than she felt. "But I have no plans to sell the island. It's my home."

The gray eyes gleamed knowingly across the table at her. Hausmann was in his element. This was his game. No one said yes to an initial offer, and he wouldn't have it any other way. He'd shown her the color of his money and now it was her job to feign disinterest and force him higher.

For a moment Annabel was tempted to play chicken, but she held herself firmly in check. What did she have to prove to men like Hausmann? She had left that world behind three years ago when she had inherited Moon Island. Impulsively, she slid the leather folder back across the table. "There's no point in continuing this discussion, Mr. Hausmann. Moon Island is not for sale."

He grinned, shark-like. "Everything is for sale, Annabel . . . and everybody."

"Perhaps where you come from," she said with a trace of bitterness.

He shrugged. "Take it, read it . . . that's all I ask. If you won't change your mind, I can accept that. I'm a reasonable man."

Rising, Annabel gathered up the folder and forced herself to shake his outstretched hand. "Very well, Mr. Hausmann. I'll read it. But my answer won't change. I'm not selling the island and that's final."

CHAPTER FOUR

Dawn waded listlessly along the waterline of Hibiscus Bay. The sun swam high above, the air was dry and hot and breathless. Although she'd only been up for a couple of hours, she felt exhausted. She hadn't eaten, it was too hot for food. Instead she'd gulped down four glasses of coconut milk and still she was thirsty. Halting to catch her breath, she slapped the surface of the water dejectedly with her walking stick. These days she was so unfit. After six months without proper exercise, it was all she could do to take a stroll along the beach.

When she finally reached the southern end of the bay, Dawn collapsed beneath a group of palm trees. Her legs were throbbing, especially below her left knee where the messiest fracture had occurred. Protruding thin and naked from her shorts, the legs scarcely seemed to belong to her. The muscles had wasted and her skin was still mottled and faintly yellowish, the legacy of massive bruising. Long angry scars ran like zippers down each thigh. The surrounding flesh felt numb and dead.

Determined not to cry, she propped herself against a husky palm trunk and took a long grateful swig from her water flask. She was screwing the top on when a voice nearby inquired, "May I have a sip of that too?"

After a start of fright, Dawn craned around to locate the source.

A woman emerged from behind the next palm tree. She was tall and slim, with the kind of fine, straight coppery hair usually associated with pale skin and freckles. Only this woman was very tanned. Surveying Dawn with eyes that also seemed too dark for her coloring, she said, "I'm sorry, did I frighten you?"

"It's okay." Avoiding her piercing glance, Dawn mechanically handed over the flask and watched the stranger drink.

She wore cotton drill shorts, slouch hat, and a white cotton shirt with the sleeves rolled up. Over this was a loose vest with dozens of pockets which all appeared to be bulging with mysterious contents. It seemed an odd choice for a day at the beach.

Perhaps realizing how out of place she looked, the woman produced a slightly lopsided smile as she returned the flask. "I'm Grace Ramsay. And yes, I'm here working." Her voice was low and slightly English-sounding.

Dawn wished there were some way of avoiding the formality of exchanging names. God only knew where it would lead. The woman was probably staying somewhere nearby. Maybe she would expect to form one of those sordid holiday friendships where people confide all sorts of intimate information, knowing that they'll never see each other again. Dawn needed that like a redback in her bra. But noting the stranger's expectant expression, she mumbled resignedly, "I'm Dawn Beaumont."

"You're Australian?"

"I'm from Sydney."

"Are you staying around here?" That candid gaze moved slowly over her body, halting at her legs.

Dawn felt as if she'd just been touched instead of looked at. Blushing, she reached for her cane. What a dumb question. Of course she was staying here. Why else would she be wandering along the beach on some desert island miles from civilization?

Something of her scorn must have showed, because the copper-haired woman gave another of those lopsided grins. "Blinding glimpse of the obvious, huh?"

Her smile was so engaging that Dawn returned it despite herself. "I'm staying over there," she said, pointing back along the bay. "In Frangipani Cottage."

"Really? You're my neighbor then. I'm only five minutes' walk from you."

"Great," Dawn said flatly. At least now she knew

which track to avoid. She'd come to this place for peace and quiet. The last thing she felt like was meaningless chitchat with inquisitive strangers.

Conscious of Grace Ramsay's scrutiny, she pulled herself clumsily to her feet and, leaning on her stick, brushed the sand off her shorts. Grace Ramsay was not as tall as Dawn had first thought. Her straight, athletic posture simply gave that impression.

From behind the safety of her shades, Dawn examined her more closely. She really was quite striking, and she looked like the type who knew it too. There was something about her — an unnerving self-awareness. It was then that she noticed the earring: a diamond stud beaming expensive light from one of Grace's earlobes. Apart from an oversized wristwatch, it was the only jewelry she wore.

As Dawn gazed, Grace lifted a hand to twist the diamond stud. "Drop in some time for coffee," she said. "I'd like to see you again."

Dawn's stomach chose that moment to pitch sharply and she lifted accusing eyes to the sun. She was feeling breathless and light-headed. Maybe she'd taken too many painkillers that morning. Shifting the weight off her heels, she tried to remember. One Voltarin and four Panadol. Yes, she really needed to cut down. Perspiration was gathering around her nose and forehead. She slid a hand inside the rim of her hat to wipe it away.

Grace Ramsay's eyes narrowed slightly at the gesture. "Are you all right?"

"I'm fine, thank you," Dawn said coolly. The

woman was giving her the jitters. Strangers often had that effect these days. It took such an effort to make them feel comfortable.

"I could walk with you," Grace offered.

Dawn took a quick pace back, shaking her head. "I'm okay."

"If you say so." Something in those charcoal eyes. A detached amusement irritated Dawn — "Well, I'll be seeing you then," Grace added, still leaning casually against the tree trunk. "Soon, I hope."

Relieved to be by herself once more, Dawn limped along Hibiscus Bay. What did the woman mean? *Soon, I hope.* She glanced apprehensively over her shoulder, then dismissed the conversation from her mind. The beach was deserted. It would have been easy to imagine she was the only person on the whole island. Heaving a pent-up sigh, she flopped down onto the sand and pulled off her sweaty shorts and top.

Her skin tingled pleasantly as the sun dried the moisture from its surface. Dawn subjected her bikini to a cursory inspection. She should put it on, she supposed, but swimming naked was one of the few things she had enjoyed about her last stay on Moon Island. There were nude beaches in Australia, of course, but parading about in front of an audience was not her idea of a good time.

Occasionally she felt dismayed at her self-consciousness. It was crazy for a swimmer to have a hang-up about showing off her body. When she was training, she virtually lived in a swimsuit, but that was different somehow.

At the beach men were such pervs, even the decent ones. If you wanted to be left alone, you had to swim at Tamarama, where they were all too busy looking at one another. Or come to places like this, of course. Flexing her ruined legs, Dawn was suddenly relieved that men were banned from Moon Island. She would be able to wear shorts the whole time she was here. Or nothing at all . . .

Reassuring herself with another quick glance along the beach, she returned her bikini to her bag and set about plaiting her hair into a thick braid. It sat hot and heavy on her neck, and for a split second she imagined it gone, cut boyishly short like that woman Grace's. No, it was ridiculous. She'd had long hair ever since she could remember. It suited her. Besides, men liked it that way.

Dawn clambered to her feet and dropped her stick on top of her clothes. It was strange walking without it, like balancing on a wall, scared to look down in case she fell. Trying not to feel insecure, she forced her eyes off her feet and began a cautious gait along the beach. Hibiscus Bay was exactly as she had always imagined Robinson Crusoe's beach might be: timeless, exotic, impossibly tranquil. The sand beneath her feet was hot and yielding, and out beyond the lagoon a coral reef shimmered like a pink mirage beneath the surface.

Dawn waded into the sea until she was buoyed off her feet. Drifting a few yards with the gentle current, she rolled onto her back, closed her eyes and lost herself in the hollow glub of bubbles rising.

The water was warm and soothing. With a small murmur of contentment, she rested her hands on her stomach. It was flat and firm. She moved to her breasts and cupped them experimentally. They were slightly smaller than usual; she'd lost a lot of weight since the accident. In fact her whole body felt light and brittle. Dawn had never realized how much she took her physical strength for granted until it was taken from her. It was scary.

She guessed her mother's force-feeding routine was a response to the change. She'd been living at home ever since she got out of hospital. What a nightmare. Her parents just didn't seem to realize that she wasn't thirteen anymore, she didn't have to go to church or have the lights out at nine o'clock. They lived in a shrine that consisted of cups, ribbons and newspaper cuttings of their champion daughter. One reporter had been so confused by the way they talked about her, he'd thought she was dead.

Thank God her mother wasn't here, Dawn thought, kicking out tentatively. It wasn't the first time she'd swum since the accident. Once the plaster was off, her physiotherapy had involved daily exercise in a pool. She'd done routines in a group, everyone grunting and complaining. Down at the other end were the paraplegics — just in case her own group thought *they* had a problem.

Initially Dawn had been thrilled when she'd finished the hospital program. All those maimed bodies, people staggering along on artificial limbs, the constant cries of pain and frustration. Who needed it? Yet she missed her particular group of friends. In the orthopedic ward, they'd been in adjoining beds, and with nothing better to do than eat, sleep, read, and watch the soaps, they'd spent most of their time talking.

There was Delia, the secretary whose woman boss sent her flowers twice a week and paid the singing telegram people to come and cheer her up; Monique with the three kids and the slob of a husband she wanted to leave; Jane whose fiancé came every day after work with chocolates, then ate them himself because she was on a diet.

Dawn had never talked so much with other women in her whole life. It was so much easier without men around. They could discuss anything they liked — sex, politics, their families. She had started to view those women as her only real friends, the only people who understood what she was going through.

After the accident, she'd had numerous visitors, of course. But once the novelty wore off, only her parents and Trish came regularly. Everyone else had their own lives to lead, she supposed. Still, it hurt sometimes to read about things her former teammates did and to realize she hadn't seen any of them for weeks.

Trying not to dwell on it, Dawn began an idle over-arm, pausing occasionally to mark herself against the bright shape of her towel. To her surprise, she swam the entire length of the bay, picking up speed as she got into her stroke. She was almost reluctant to stop, but common sense dictated that she slow down while she was still strong enough to swim ashore.

Feeling ridiculously proud of herself, she switched to a modest breaststroke, only to have her delight quickly fade. Her legs were generating virtually no push at all. She couldn't even get them in time with each other. Overwhelmed with dismay, she shook the water from her eyes and flipped onto her back, allowing the sea to cradle her.

It really was true, she thought bitterly. She'd crashed that car, killed her teammate and destroyed her own swimming career, all for the sake of a few drinks with Nigel Myers. Tears merged with the salt water washing her temples, and she squinted up at the empty sky. Eventually something brushed her back and she connected gently with sand. For a few long moments, she succumbed to the balmy caresses of the breaking tide, then she got to her feet and looked around for her towel.

It was way down the beach. Served her right for getting distracted, she thought wryly. She'd only limped a few paces toward it when she was gripped by the same curious light-headedness she'd experienced an hour or so ago while talking to the copper-haired woman. Shaking her head, she proceeded more slowly. It was no good. Her legs felt like cooked spaghetti and all of a sudden the beach lurched before her.

Why hadn't she listened to Cody and Annabel's warnings about the sun, Dawn thought miserably. Why was she always so pig-headed? Head spinning, she ventured another a small step. The sand swayed and undulated front of her. Blood was rushing in her ears. Overhead, gulls lamented. Dawn stared up at them, watching a bird soar higher and higher. Then her eyes closed against the impossible brightness of the sun and she didn't even feel her face hit the sand.

* * * * *

Dawn had no idea how much time had passed when she blinked up into a dark, concerned stare.

"I'm going to get you into some shade," Grace Ramsay said in her low clipped tone. "Put your arms around my neck."

Dawn hesitated, but the arm supporting her shoulders had already tightened and another slid beneath her knees. "It's okay" — that teasing smile — "I won't drop you."

Dawn felt so weak she could only rest her head against Grace's shoulder. There was something comforting about being cradled that way, immersed in a mixture of scents — salt, skin, sun on cotton, some kind of spicy perfume.

At the edge of the jungle, Grace lowered Dawn onto the sandy earth, commenting, "I think you've had too much sun." Her arm was still loosely around Dawn's waist and her face was very close. She had long straight black eyelashes and her eyes were the color of wet stones, tiny flecks of green banding the iris.

Dawn stared. She couldn't help herself.

Toying with her earring, Grace stared back. "I see you're a natural blonde," she said softly.

Dawn's cheeks burned. She was completely naked, she remembered. And Grace Ramsay was looking her up and down, calm as you please. Mortified, Dawn wriggled upright. Her limbs felt glutinous. "Please, get my clothes," she stammered.

An infuriating grin twitched the corners of Grace's mouth, but she rose obediently and sauntered across the sand to collect the discarded bag.

Dawn could hardly believe her eyes. It was that walk. The one she hated. The calm swagger she associated irrevocably with Cody Stanton. When Grace returned, Dawn raised an arm to cover her breasts.

The protective gesture only seemed to amuse Grace. "Don't let it bother you, Dawn," she said, dark eyes hinting at insolence. "I've seen it all before."

What was that supposed to mean? Lobbing her most withering look at the stranger, Dawn dragged on her clothes and knotted her belt with shaking fingers. She didn't like Grace Ramsay, she decided. There was something about her attitude.

Seemingly impervious, Grace said, "I think I'd better walk you home."

"That won't be necessary," Dawn snapped.

Grace looked unmoved. "That's what you thought last time. I think I'll tag along just in case. Can you walk okay? Or would you like me to carry you?"

Vehemently Dawn shook her head. "I said I can manage. See?" She scrambled to feet to prove it. "I'm perfectly all right."

Grace's eyes flickered with growing impatience. "Are you always so rude and defensive about your disability, Dawn?" she drawled. "Or have you just taken a particular dislike to me?"

Dawn studied her feet. She was being rude and unreasonable, she supposed. It was no way to treat a stranger whose worst crime was trying to help her. If she had any sense, she would accept Grace's offer and be thankful. Ashamed, she wriggled her toes, noticing the chipped crimson polish. Too bad, she thought recklessly. Once upon a time she was very picky about personal grooming, but now that she didn't have to impress anyone anymore ...

She lifted reluctant eyes. "I'm sorry I snapped at you," she managed. "I just ... I'm not feeling very well ..."

Grace subjected her to a cool, measuring stare. "We're all entitled to an off day." Then she smiled, all charm and nonchalance.

It took far too long to reach the cottage. The path through the jungle was well trodden but narrow, and the effort of pushing aside the thickly interwoven creepers tired Dawn quickly. Watching Grace stroll easily ahead of her, she wondered what it was about the woman that got under her skin.

Dawn guessed she was about thirty. At a glance she looked younger, somewhat boyish. It was a fashionable look, the short hair, long legs, distinct shoulder muscles. Dawn's eyes were drawn to the neat roll of her hips and she found herself thinking about Cody Stanton again. Grace had the same kind of streetwise air about her. Dawn recalled a conversation she'd had with one of the women staying on the island the last time she was here. Sexy. That was what she'd called Cody.

Bothered, she forced her eyes off the woman in front of her. Maybe they'd gone to the same deportment classes. Or maybe ... she fled from the idea. She didn't want to think about the fact that Cody Stanton was a lesbian.

They were nearing the cottage. It was set on a slight rise on the northeastern face of the island. Before the hurricane three years ago, it had been the only dwelling on this part of the island and was surrounded by old frangipani trees. Hurricane Mary and its attendant tsunami had devastated both house and gardens, leaving a trail of uprooted trees and a mere shell where the cottage had stood.

The new cottage was built farther back from the ocean for protection from the tidal waves that had claimed its predecessor, and a second cottage had been constructed at the same time, even farther inland.

New gardens had been planted, and in the fecundity of the tropics they had quickly overtaken the scars left by the hurricane. Looking at Frangipani Cottage now, it was difficult to imagine any other landscape. Lush greenery surrounded the place, teeming with insects and bird life, bougainvillea meandered across the veranda, and everything smelled green and moist.

Halting at the veranda, Grace propped herself against a wooden pillar, removing her hat to fan herself indolently. Her hair was bright in the afternoon sun, and feathered damply onto her forehead. With a combination of guilt and annoyance, Dawn dragged herself up the whitewashed steps. Now that they were here she supposed the least she could do was offer her visitor a glass of water or something.

Catching a hint of challenge in Grace's expression, she grudgingly offered, "Would you like a cup of tea." Maybe Grace would have other plans.

Evidently not. In the kitchen she removed her

vest and suspended it casually over the back of a chair. The movement parted her white shirt where it was unbuttoned, and Dawn caught a glimpse of tanned breast and dark nipple. Hastily she turned to the little gas stove, and after several futile attempts, managed to light the burner. Grace Ramsay went without a bra. So what? This was Moon Island. There was no one to see. Except women.

Dawn deposited the cups on the table. She was absurdly conscious of Grace's bold dark eyes following her every movement. Was the woman trying to make her nervous?

"You're on holiday alone?" Grace asked in a conversational tone.

Dawn mumbled a yes. The water still wasn't boiling. She fidgeted beside the stove.

"Me too," Grace said. "It's a great place to come for some time out. How long are you staying?"

"Three weeks," Dawn admitted.

"So am I." Grace glanced wryly at her vest. "I wish I had more free time to enjoy the place."

Determined to avoid drawing out the visit, Dawn refrained from asking what exactly Grace did. Once this was over, she reminded herself, she would have made her concession to good manners. She wouldn't need to see her neighbor again. To her relief the water was finally boiling. She slopped it carelessly into the teapot.

"What part of Sydney are you from?" Grace asked.

"My family lives in Randwick."

"I worked in Sydney a few years back." When Dawn did not respond, Grace volunteered, "I'm a scientist."

41

Her tone was matter-of-fact, as though there was nothing at all unusual in this revelation, as though a woman scientist was as commonplace and unspectacular as a nurse or a receptionist.

Dawn felt slightly piqued, but curious too. "Is that what you're doing here on the island ... something scientific?"

"You could say that." Grace's eyes became guarded all of a sudden. "I'm writing a report on coral reef structures in the South Pacific." She went on to describe some research project she was involved in. None of the technical terms made any sense to Dawn.

"It sounds fascinating," Dawn lied.

"I'm enjoying it." Grace gave a teasing smile, as if she knew Dawn found the very idea boring and incomprehensible. "I'm usually based in New York, but I get to travel all over."

"Who do you work for?"

Again the hesitation. "I work on contract, usually for big international companies."

She sounded uncomfortable. Perhaps she was embarrassed about being so successful, Dawn conjectured. Grace was obviously one of those tough, clever women who negotiated highly paid assignments for themselves all over the world. She wasn't stuck in the suburbs minding kids for a bunch of Westies while they went to their boring jobs.

Dawn glanced at Grace's fingers. They were long and expressive. No wedding ring; not even the telltale mark of one recently discarded. Obviously Grace didn't have a man to wait on when she got home. She probably lived alone in some big

42

impractical apartment with cream-colored everything. She probably ate out for every meal. She probably owned her own sports car ...

Swallowing a sigh, Dawn got a grip on herself. What did she care how Grace Ramsay lived?

Grace was getting to her feet and again Dawn noticed the way her shirt dragged across her small high breasts, her dark nipples pressed against the fabric. She wished she wasn't so fascinated by the sight. What on earth was the matter with her? Was she noticing other women's bodies all of a sudden because hers was ruined?

Quite suddenly she felt exhausted. Stifling a yawn, she followed Grace out onto the veranda and stood beside her, taking in the view across the jungle to the sea. The air was tinted with some scent. Cloves. It was quite delicious. For a second Dawn wondered dreamily if it was some exotic plant in her garden, then she traced the source to Grace's shirt, remembering that smell from earlier in the day.

Grace was gazing at her oddly. It was almost as though she were asking something. "Thanks for the tea," she said.

Confused, Dawn managed a half-hearted smile. "Um ... thanks for walking me home." It felt awkward, the two of them standing there on the veranda, being so polite.

Grace twisted her earring. "Well, I'll see you again." She touched Dawn's arm for a fleeting second. Warmth flooded Dawn's cheeks and her skin prickled under Grace's fingers.

It was only after she'd watched Grace saunter into the jungle that Dawn realized she had been holding her breath. Taking a sharp, shallow gulp of air, she retreated indoors and sought out her bed. A long time later, staring up at her ceiling, she was engulfed by a clamoring uneasiness. Would she see the overly friendly Grace Ramsay again? Not if she could help it.

CHAPTER FIVE

It was late afternoon when Dawn awoke from her nap. Drowsily, she rolled onto her back, swallowing the clean fragrant air and listening to the jumbled cacophony beyond her window. The jungle was never quiet; you could almost hear it growing. The sounds of pre-dusk were busy, chaotic, signaling the sun's impending demise. Insects chirped relentlessly, frogs croaked, and all over the island creatures recovered from the heat of the day and bustled home, foraging for final tidbits on the way.

It was so different from the city. No horns

blaring, traffic whining, radios, TVs, hordes of people. Just the ever-present pulse of the ocean and the comforting *sotto voce* of nature at work.

Dawn left her bed and wandered out to the kitchen, staring disconsolately at the used cups still sitting on the table. She should make a meal, she thought. But she wasn't particularly hungry. Pouring a large glass of pineapple juice, she dragged herself out onto the veranda and flopped into a deep cane chair.

She could always read a book. She'd brought a pile of paperbacks with her.

Or she could write a letter . . .

Dear Nigel.

How is training coming along? Thank you for the flowers. I'm having a holiday in the Cook Islands. I'll phone you when I get back.

Or would she? Nigel hadn't exactly broken records to sit at her bedside. What did she expect anyway? They'd only dated a few times, yet somehow Nigel had meant more to her than any of the other men at the club. He'd always given his mates the impression that there was something between them.

He was busy, of course. Olympic selection was only months away and he could still improve his times. She was a sportswoman; she could understand that imperative. Knotting her fingers behind her head, she sought comfort in her exercise routine. Lift, flex and stretch, flex and stretch.

It was no good. She couldn't avoid thinking about it. Even now, six months later, it barely felt real. It had all happened so fast. Someone had offered her a ride home but she'd said no. She had her own car and besides, Nigel had asked her to stay for another drink. Two glasses later he was asking her to come home with him and Dawn was groping for an excuse to decline. She was taking Lynda, she'd said. Someone always had to drop Lynda off; she didn't drive.

Nigel had been surly. He had a right to be, she supposed. She had been saying no to him for months, and she wasn't even sure why. That night he had called her a frigid tease and one or two other insulting things, and she'd driven off in a rage. She hadn't even seen the corner. Even now she couldn't remember what had happened. One minute Lynda was asking her to slow down and the next she was lying on a bed, a drip feeding into her arm and a nurse shining a torch in her eyes.

Dawn swallowed the lump in her throat. There was no point in reliving the past. What's done is done, she told herself. Then she started to cry in earnest.

She was still sitting there, head in her hands, when a familiar voice inquired, "Dawn?"

She jerked upright, meeting a pair of quizzical gray eyes. "Oh, it's you."

Cody Stanton took in her tear-stained face then sat, uninvited, in the other cane chair.

She looked so relaxed and happy that Dawn felt like hitting her. "Go away," she mumbled resentfully.

Cody stayed where she was. "Do you want to talk about it, Dawn?" She reached out and took one of Dawn's hands.

"No, I don't." Dawn snatched her hand away as though scalded. "It's none of your business."

"Dawn," Cody persisted. "I might be able to help you if you'd let me." Moving to Dawn's chair, she crouched beside her, adding quietly, "I know you and I have never got along. And I know you don't like me or approve of the way I live, but . . ."

Dawn looked at Cody. "That's not true," she whispered, suddenly conscious of color flooding her cheeks.

For a split second Cody's face registered confusion, then her expression relaxed into its usual easygoing charm. "Then how about coming back to Villa Luna with me now," she coaxed. "Annabel's making something yummy for dinner. We could just get drunk and reminisce about hurricanes . . . if you don't want to talk about what happened."

Even as Dawn opened her mouth to decline, she found herself responding to Cody's enthusiasm with a small, watery smile.

Her visitor instantly read this as acceptance. "Great. Go get your stuff and I'll wait for you out here."

Torn between irritation and gratitude, Dawn dragged herself out of the armchair. Once upon a time, she would have told Cody to go away, then sat about feeling sorry for herself for the rest of the night. But right now, she didn't feel like being a martyr. She vacillated for a moment longer then shrugged. "I hope you're not expecting me to walk," she said.

It was worse than that.

Their transport was tethered beneath a palm tree and snorted at her as Cody tightened its saddle.

Dawn nearly turned around and went straight

back inside. "I can't do this," she protested as Cody helped her into the saddle. "I don't know how to ride."

"But I do." Cody swung up behind her and reached around, placing Dawn's hands firmly on a raised leather mound in front of her. "That's called the pommel. Just hang on to it and leave the rest to me and Kahlo."

Protesting volubly, Dawn made a grab for the saddle as they plunged into the jungle. They seemed awfully high up and the black horse was pulling at the reins and tossing its head like a wild animal.

"She's very spirited today," Cody commented, stretching past Dawn to pat the dark muscular neck.

"Terrific. Black Beauty runs amok."

"Relax." Cody was infuriatingly blasé. "You might even enjoy it. Besides, if she senses you're nervous, she'll give you a hard time."

Dawn sighed, but she made a conscious attempt to reduce the tension in her muscles. The only problem with that was how close it brought her to Cody. Suddenly she was acutely conscious of the arms on either side of her, the press of Cody's thighs, her body warm and close. For one appalling moment she felt herself relaxing against Cody, then her mind fastened onto the memory of Cody and Annabel kissing on Passion Bay, and she straightened sharply. Her mouth was as dry as dust and there was a peculiar gnawing in the pit of her stomach.

"Are you comfortable?" Cody's breath grazed her cheek.

Dawn nodded mutely. What on earth was the matter with her? With bizarre fascination, she stared at Cody's arms, at the hands controlling the reins. She was overcome by a powerful urge to touch her, stroke her, nestle against her. Disbelief clouded her consciousness like a swarm of wasps. She was attracted to Cody. No! It couldn't be true!

Hunching forward, she clutched the pommel with sweaty fingers. Of course it wasn't true. It was her imagination; the aftermath of sunstroke. And the drugs, of course, had all sorts of odd side effects. Dawn ordered herself to breathe and stay calm. No, she couldn't possibly be attracted to Cody. Cody was a woman. And not just a woman, she reminded herself hastily, a *lesbian*.

Annabel met them on the veranda of Villa Luna. She looked like a film star, Dawn thought, fighting off a stab of envy. She hung back as Cody planted a kiss squarely on her lover's mouth, then led Kahlo off.

"I'm so glad you could come." Annabel greeted her with every indication of pleasure and showed her inside. "I can't believe it's been nearly three years since you were here."

"Neither can I." Dawn sank into a chair. Watching Annabel pour their drinks, she tried not to think about her and Cody.

Annabel handed her a glass and sat down on the sofa opposite, smoothing her bright blue sarong across her thighs. She was wearing her hair loose, and it spilled fine and silky across her pale shoulders.

Dawn gazed at her curiously. Annabel was the

only albino she'd ever seen close up, and she was astonished at the whiteness of her hair and skin. How on earth did she manage to avoid getting burnt, living out here on an island? It wasn't as if she stayed indoors all the time.

"Do you live out here all year round?" she asked, taking a prolonged drink and licking her lips with pleasure. The cocktail was wonderful, a mixture of coconut milk and tropical fruit juice.

"Not quite," Annabel said. "We visit Cody's mother in New Zealand quite often and we spend several months of the year at my place in Boston."

"Otherwise Annabel suffers shopping withdrawal," teased a voice from the doorway. Cody wandered into the room, poured herself a drink, and sat down beside Annabel, resting a casual hand on her knee.

Dawn studied her drink. You'd think they could be more discreet instead of flaunting their relationship so blatantly. It was downright embarrassing. Lifting censorious eyes, she intercepted a look that passed between them, a look of such undiluted passion that her mouth went dry with shock. They were besotted with each other. Hopelessly in love. And it seemed so natural . . .

Dawn shook herself, forced her thoughts to Nigel and tried to envisage having feelings like that for him, for anyone . . . It was useless. She couldn't begin to imagine it. Maybe she was a shallow person. Maybe she would never experience true love, never share with anyone whatever it was that Cody and Annabel had. She probably wouldn't recognize the emotion if she fell over it.

Her attention was drawn again to the two women and all of a sudden she found herself envying them bitterly, forgetting they weren't normal. They just looked so happy. Tears of self-pity stung her eyes. Dawn rubbed them impatiently aside and looked up to find Cody watching her.

"Dawn, what is it?"

"Nothing." She folded defensive arms across her stomach. "I'm just tired."

Annabel was staring too, those strange lavender eyes wide and concerned. "Have you had too much sun? You're looking quite ill."

"No. I'm fine. Honestly."

"Maybe you should lie down before dinner," Annabel continued. "I'll get you an aspirin ..."

"No!" Dawn bit her lip. She hadn't meant to sound so hostile, but a terrible anger was swelling inside her. She wanted to smash her glass and scream at the world that there was no God because a God with any decency would never have done this to her.

Abruptly, she got to her feet and paced to the open window. She was cracking up, she thought with a surge of panic. They would put her on lithium next, like one of the women in her hospital ward, and she would turn into a zombie. Lifting trembling fingers to her forehead, she stared out at the sky. It was awash with vivid, shifting colors, orange, cerise, pink and gold. Distracted by its astounding beauty, she watched the procession of colors from sapphire through heliotrope then to amethyst, until finally the bloodred sun fused with the ocean.

Conscious then of the other women, she said dully, "It's my legs. They hurt sometimes and I'm trying to cut down on my painkillers."

A jumpy silence followed.

"Was it a car accident?" Cody asked eventually.

To Dawn's horror she felt tears streaming down her face and her shoulders began to shake uncontrollably. "It's the worst thing that's ever happened to me," she cried harshly. "I wish I were dead!"

Cody crossed the room and gently took Dawn in her arms. For a long time the two women stood there, Dawn sobbing and Cody rubbing her back and making soothing noises.

"I don't know what to do," Dawn wept. "I've lost everything. I'll never swim again and I was training for the Olympic trials. I just can't believe it . . ." She wiped her face with her arm, suddenly appalled at breaking down in front of these women. Backing out of Cody's embrace, she sagged against the window frame. "Oh what does it matter," she said bleakly. "Forget it. It's my problem, not yours."

"Dawn." Annabel approached, a box of Kleenex in her hand. "Please don't punish yourself for needing support."

Dawn took the tissues. The kindness in Annabel's voice only made her more upset. Annabel was being nice to her, after all the things she had thought about her and Cody. Paralyzed with shame, she looked up, caught the shimmer of tears in Annabel's eyes, and cried even harder. She barely noticed being led out onto the veranda and eased gently into the deep two-seater overlooking the ocean.

After a long silence, Annabel spoke. "Isn't it beautiful." She was gazing out across Passion Bay.

Dawn stared too. It was breathtaking. The moon hung in the night sky like a well-polished tin, staining the ocean quicksilver. The air was warm

53

and sultry, scented with the crush of tropical leaves and flowers. "I remember this view," she hiccuped. "I used to sit out here night after night when we were waiting to be rescued."

Back then she had always thought she was just keeping watch for the steamer. But it was much more than that, she realized with a flash of understanding. Looking out across Passion Bay, you couldn't help but feel a sense of belonging, of being part of the miracle of life.

Annabel was smiling contentedly. "I think this is my favorite place on earth. Whenever I'm away from here I feel like I'm serving a prison sentence. I just can't wait to get back." She laughed as though amused at herself. "And to think, I used to be such a city girl."

Meeting her eyes, Dawn realized she was alone with Annabel. Where was Cody?

Annabel must have read her mind. "I've put Cody to work in the kitchen. Hopefully, any minute we'll be summoned to a delicious meal. I don't think she's had time to burn it."

Dawn blew her nose. "I feel really stupid about this."

"There's no need," Annabel said. "As far as I'm concerned you can cry all you want while you're with us."

"I've done enough crying." Dawn twisted her hands in her lap. "It's time I got my act together. I have to do something with my life. I just feel stuck. All I ever wanted was to swim."

"Surely that couldn't last forever. What were you planning to do once you'd retired?"

"I've never given it much thought. I guess I had vague ideas about coaching. And I figured I'd get married someday, have kids. But . . ."

Annabel raised her eyebrows. "But?"

Dawn gave a harsh little laugh. "Well, look at me. I can't even walk properly. My legs look like they've been run over by a lawn mower and my hands too. Who's going to marry me now?"

"Was there someone . . ."

"Nobody special," Dawn responded gruffly, her thoughts straying to Nigel. "I mean, we weren't engaged or anything."

Annabel's expression was cautious. "Are you still seeing him?"

Dawn studied her feet, unsure how to answer. She never really was *seeing* him, was she? "He's been busy." Knowing she sounded defensive, she paused to clear her throat. "He's a finalist for Olympic selection."

Annabel nodded as if she understood. She seemed about to say something else when Cody appeared with the news that dinner was served and that this time she hadn't burnt the sauce.

"Don't straight women have complicated lives," Cody mumbled a long time later, snuggling into Annabel in the sleepy darkness.

Annabel kissed her cheek. "We all have our share of problems. Ours are just different from theirs."

"It sounds like he dumped her." Cody sighed disgustedly. "What a prince."

55

"She's pretending it doesn't matter," Annabel said. "But I don't think it's done much for her self-esteem."

"Well, that's the trouble with buying into men's beauty standards. You're stuffed unless you measure up."

"You know," Annabel mused, "I get the distinct impression that underneath it all Dawn's not that stuck on men."

Cody laughed. "You don't know the woman, sweetheart! You didn't have to spend forty-eight hours trapped in a cave with her. All she could talk about was men. And she's a raving homophobe."

"That doesn't mean anything. She could be latent."

Cody groaned. "Lesbian reality strikes again. Every woman is a dyke. Honestly, Annabel, you're straight out of the seventies sometimes."

Annabel prodded her playfully in the ribs. "Okay smart-ass. Then maybe you can explain how come Dawn has such a huge crush on you if she's so super-straight."

Cody stiffened. "What do you mean?"

"Observant, aren't we? Don't tell me you haven't noticed. She only stares at you all the time and blushes when you speak to her."

"Straight woman often get jumpy around me," Cody said. "You don't get so much of that kind of thing because you look so . . ."

"So what?" Annabel made a grab for Cody as she tried to escape beneath the covers. "You were going to say safe, weren't you? Passing?"

"No I wasn't." Cody fended her off. "I was going to say . . . er . . . pretty. Beautiful . . ." Her arms slid around Annabel and she lifted her hair to kiss the nape of her neck. "Absolutely ravishing . . ."

"Don't think you can sweet-talk me." Annabel slapped her hands away. "You're evading the whole issue. Dawn Beaumont definitely has a crush on you."

Cody sighed dramatically. "And you read too many Naiads."

"We'll see," Annabel murmured with prim conviction. She thought about Dawn recovering from a traumatic accident, emotionally vulnerable and confused about her sexuality. It was a volatile combination. For a brief crazy second she panicked at what it might lead to. She hoped Cody would tread carefully. Otherwise they could be in for three very uncomfortable weeks.

CHAPTER SIX

Grace awoke sweating and disoriented. Whitewashed walls surrounded her, cool and grayish in
the half-light. Drawn by the large open window
above her bed, she slowly focused on the view it
framed, listened for the sounds that anchored her to
reality. There was only stillness, the mystical calm
that foretells the coming of dawn, that pause when
every living creature seems to hold its breath before
saluting the day. As she lay unmoving, the eerie
moment passed. A bird cried, a pale green streak of

light traversed the sky, and a morning breeze stirred the ocean's face.

Tension dissolving, Grace pushed off her bedclothes and stretched. A peculiar image was repeating itself in her consciousness. The face of an animal, a dog. She frowned. She had never owned a dog, only cats. One cat. Missy. She had died four years ago and Grace had decided then never to have another pet.

She must have dreamed about the dog. How odd. Normally she never remembered anything about the Dream. She only knew that she'd had it. She always woke paralyzed. Grace felt disturbed. Was she remembering something after all this time? Her therapist had said it was bound to happen one day and the sooner the better, so she could "deal with it." Grace hadn't agreed. She wasn't about to spend years in therapy feeling sorry for herself and using the past as an excuse for avoiding the future. Instead she had worked her ass off to carve out a decent career and to earn her black belt in karate.

Rejecting her unsettling train of thought, Grace showered and brushed her teeth. Being a victim was a state of mind, nothing more, she reminded herself She was physically strong and had money and assets and a job with status. No one could take those things away from her.

An hour later she was chopping papaw and bananas into a bowl. Adding thick coconut cream, she carried her breakfast out onto the veranda. Her cottage looked out across Hibiscus Bay, a picture-book setting, skirted by lush, tropical greenery, waving palms and brightly hued cannas and hibiscus.

For a moment Grace was sorry she couldn't simply relax and enjoy it. But she wasn't here for a holiday. She had less than three weeks to complete a full feasibility study on the conversion of the island to a toxic waste disposal site.

So far it looked promising. Moon Island was the most isolated of the Cook group. It was ideal: far enough away from civilization to attract a minimum of attention and large enough to support the kind of facilities required. There was little chance of tourists stumbling on the place by accident, and hopefully Greenpeace would have better things to do raising money and saving seals than to hound a company engaging in legitimate business activity.

Argus was prepared to pay handsomely for a foothold in the region and according to Robert Hausmann, the Cook Islands' Premier was falling over backwards to accommodate them. That was hardly surprising, Grace thought with a measure of cynicism. She could imagine Argus landing the company jet at Avarua, Hausmann touring the place, endowing a hospital, building a school. Gestures of goodwill.

With Hausmann handling the purchase of Moon Island, it was Grace's job to come up with recommendations for establishing deep-water access and appropriate dumping protocols. They couldn't risk destroying the reef entirely. It provided the perfect solution to the problem of pollution. A reef could easily be landfilled with nontoxic waste, and toxic materials confined to the island itself. And unlike the Marshalls, the Cook Islands weren't likely to be affected by contaminants carried downwind of the dumping zone. That was exactly the kind of embarrassing problem a reputable company like Argus took pains to avoid.

So far she had assessed the impact on the island of blasting away a portion of its coral reef to establish a passable channel, and she was now calculating the total landfill capacity. Glancing through her report data, Grace made a few notes, then dropped the papers on the small table beside her and scanned her surroundings. Somehow she couldn't work up much enthusiasm today for her job. Perhaps it was the sunshine, the distant sound of the sea.

Through the dense green foliage to her right, she could just make out the thatched roof of Frangipani Cottage. She thought about its inhabitant. Dawn, the prickly young Australian, was an unexpected but pleasant distraction. Grace smiled, recalling her nakedness, the arms across the breasts, the picture of outraged virtue. Very fetching, but not very convincing. For all the protestations, those bright blue eyes were a dead giveaway. Grace never missed a sexual cue.

Getting to her feet, she smoothed her shorts. The Australian was definitely her cup of tea. Young, cute and reassuringly shallow. The perfect fuck, no less. It was a pity about her legs. The scars looked recent, and she was obviously painfully self-conscious of them. It must be tough, Grace reflected. Dawn had probably been a real knockout before it happened. She still was, scars aside. But maybe she didn't see it that way.

For a moment Grace contemplated leaving the kid alone. She was a bit young and it seemed almost too easy. On the other hand, there was something very appealing about that mixture of arrogance and vulnerability. If Dawn was feeling as undesirable as Grace suspected, she'd be doing her a favor. Nothing like good sex to boost a woman's confidence.

Grace wondered idly how long it would take to get her neighbor into the sack. Three days? Less? Draining her coffee, she placed a bet with herself. That coveted new Vuitton trunk, if she could seduce Dawn Beaumont within forty-eight hours.

Dawn was deeply enmeshed in the latest Jackie Collins novel when she heard footsteps on her veranda. There was a knock on her door, a voice called her name.

Recognizing the clipped tone, she instantly froze in her chair. What was that woman doing here? She would pretend she wasn't home, she decided. Hopefully Grace Ramsay hadn't seen her through the big windows that opened onto the veranda. Dawn craned slightly to check. There was a loud thud. Dismayed, she stared down at the floor where her Jackie Collins was splayed open.

"Oh, there you are." A coppery head poked in the window.

Guilty heat flooded Dawn's cheeks.

"Did I wake you?" her visitor asked, swinging one

long leg over the windowsill and casually perching astride it. She was wearing baggy khaki shorts and a thin faded shirt. Beneath the brim of her slouch hat her eyes shone dark and bold.

Avoiding them, Dawn said, "I was only reading."

Grace Ramsay was here out of politeness, of course. After all, the woman had found her passed out on the beach just the day before.

Bearing out this assumption, Grace inquired, "Are you feeling better today?"

"Yes," Dawn replied. "I think it was just sunstroke. I'm fine now."

"Great." Grace smiled broadly. Dawn didn't like the way her dark eyes were glittering, as if she knew something Dawn didn't. "How about coming on a walk with me? I've even packed a picnic."

A picnic! Dawn's chest constricted and she cast distractedly about for an excuse. "No ..." She shook her head. "I don't think so ... I, er ..."

Grace swung her other leg over the sill and faced Dawn squarely. "It's a beautiful day out there," she continued in a persuasive tone. "Far too nice to shut yourself away with only Jackie Collins for company."

Dawn glanced ambivalently toward the book. Grace was right. She should be outside getting fresh air and exercise, not cooped up in her cottage doing a Greta Garbo. A picnic. It sounded harmless enough, and it was not as if she had other plans.

Stealing a covert look at Grace, she felt vaguely ashamed of herself. There was no need for her to be so standoffish. The woman was only trying to be friendly. "I guess a walk would be nice," she conceded awkwardly. "Although I can't go terribly far... I mean ... my legs ..."

"I thought we'd go inland a bit." Grace acted as if there was no problem. "There's a lookout point about half an hour away. It's quite stunning up there."

"I think I know where you mean." Dawn brightened, remembering the ridge that circled the *makatea* in the center of the island. It was a beautiful spot. She and Cody had paused up there the day before to admire the views.

"You know the island?" Grace seemed pleased.

"I've stayed here once before."

"Then you'll be able to lead the way back if I get us lost." Grace gave a quirky little smile.

Dawn got to her feet, still vaguely dubious. Her face must have betrayed something, because Grace was suddenly serious. "If you're worried about making the distance, don't be. I can always carry you if you get tired."

She was completely serious. Tensing, Dawn recalled being carried naked in Grace's arms the day before. "I'm sure that won't be necessary," she said hastily.

Again that smile. "You never know your luck."

Inland, the island was thickly covered in jungle. It smelled close and damp, and Dawn felt heady with the scents of gardenia and frangipani. Grace halted at regular intervals to take what seemed a wasteful quantity of photos. Nevertheless Dawn was glad of these frequent opportunities to rest her protesting legs. This was the first time she had attempted an uphill walk of any duration and she was amazed at how well she was managing.

"When were you here last?" Grace asked as they were climbing the ridge.

"Nearly three years ago." Dawn gripped Grace's arm as she picked her way slowly across the uneven terrain. It frustrated her to feel so dependent, but she was acutely conscious of the razor-sharp coral beneath the lush foliage.

"Have you been up on this ridge before?"

"On part of it. I've crossed the *makatea* over by Passion Bay. There are some caves in the middle of the island."

"Really?" Grace helped her over a fallen tree. "How do you get to them?"

Dawn stumbled, then tensed as Grace's hold on her tightened. As soon as she got her footing, she pulled quickly away. "You'd have to ask Cody. I only went there once. During the hurricane. We had to sleep there, taking shelter."

"With Cody? Lucky you."

The comment puzzled Dawn. "It was really scary." She shivered. "I don't like caves."

"What do you like, Dawn?" There was a roguishness about Grace's expression.

Avoiding those disquieting eyes, Dawn said, "I like music."

"Music," Grace echoed. "Me too. Have you ever been to Michigan?"

It seemed a bizarre question.

"To the Women's Music Festival," Grace elaborated.

"No, I haven't." They were almost at the top of

the rise, Dawn noted with relief And a good thing too. Her legs were on the verge of collapse.

As they cleared the ridge, Grace halted beside her, pointing at a small clearing. "There's the lookout." She helped Dawn along the ridge, easing her to the ground as they reached the grassy clearing. Then, removing her pack, she dropped down beside it, stretching her long legs out in front of her and taking off her hat to fan herself.

"Feeling okay?" She glanced at Dawn.

Dawn nodded swiftly. "Just thirsty." She pulled her water flask off her shoulder.

Grace waited for her to finish drinking, then waved an arm. "What do you think? Surreal, isn't it?"

Dawn took in the view. The huge blue circle of ocean and sky was bisected by a shimmering horizon. "Incredible. It's hard to imagine that anywhere else even exists. Perhaps the whole world was once like this . . ." She trailed off, conscious she was sounding sloppy and sentimental.

"Gondwanaland." Grace flicked her a lopsided grin. "Paradise . . . for dinosaurs at any rate." She had produced a lightweight rug from her pack and was spreading it across the ground. "Here," she invited. "Get comfortable."

After screwing the lid onto her flask, Dawn inched across to perch on the edge of the blanket. Grace gave her an odd look, then shrugged almost imperceptibly and lay down, arms behind her head, hat tilted across her face. She looked very strong, Dawn thought, eyeing the muscular legs stretched out in front of her, the solid smoothness of her arms and shoulders. Somehow Grace didn't fit Dawn's image of a scientist, which, she'd always thought, should be a small, rather gray person wearing thick glasses and a white coat.

To her embarrassment, Grace began unbuttoning her shirt, pulling it from the khaki shorts and letting it fall open. She sighed as the sun met her skin. Her breasts and torso were like the rest of her, smooth and tanned. Obviously she sunbathed like this all the time. Unable to help herself, Dawn glanced at Grace's nipples, marveling at how dark they were. She stared for a long time, her breathing strangely affected, then she dragged her attention back to the scenery.

She felt clammy. Was she going to be sick? she wondered with alarm. Had the climb been too much? Again her eyes were drawn to her companion, and her heart skipped a beat. Grace was staring straight at her.

"How old are you, Dawn?" she asked softly.

"Twenty-two."

"God, that's young." Smiling, Grace rolled onto her side and reached for her pack.

Dawn lifted her chin. "How old are you?"

"Thirty-two. And I live in New York, so that adds up to about a hundred by normal standards."

"It's that bad?"

"It depends who you are and how much money you have." Grace lifted an assortment of plastic containers from her pack. "Hungry?"

"A little bit."

To Dawn's surprise she consumed an enormous quantity of food over the next half hour.

Even Grace seemed impressed. "You don't look so pale now." She studied Dawn's face intently. "Tell me, are you involved with anyone at the moment?"

The question took Dawn by surprise, and despite the sun, her skin began to goose-bump. "No, I'm not," she replied.

"Neither am I."

Dawn hoped that was all Grace planned to say. She had no intention of getting into all that personal stuff with a stranger. In fact, she'd had quite enough of this conversation, she decided. With faltering hands, she started packing up their picnic things.

"I'll do that." Grace sat up, calmly buttoning her shirt. "Are you in some kind of hurry?"

Screening her increasing disquiet with a lame smile, Dawn said, "I don't want to spend too long in the sun. After yesterday . . ."

"Sure. I understand." Grace stuffed everything into her pack and buttoned it down. "We could go back to my place for a while. Would you like that?"

Dawn lifted her eyes, only to find them drawn relentlessly to the gap in Grace's shirt, the outline of her nipples against the thin cotton. In the grip of a peculiar fascination, she proceeded up Grace's body, pausing at the hollow of her throat, the wide sensual mouth. Then she met those dark eyes and her mouth dried.

"Is that a yes?" Grace asked.

Something in her tone made Dawn's nerves leap. Frowning, she stared at the scars on her hands. What was wrong with her? Why was she so jumpy? Unevenly, she said, "I'm feeling quite tired. I'm sorry."

"It's okay." Grace was suddenly businesslike,

gathering their belongings and passing Dawn her stick. "Maybe we came too far, huh?" Glancing at Dawn's legs, she added, "I'm the one who should be sorry, dragging you up here." She toyed with her earring. "You seemed a little down. I thought you might enjoy it."

"I did," Dawn hastened to say. "I do . . . It's just . . ." How could she explain her uneasiness? There was no logic to anything she was feeling.

Grace's expression was very intent, her eyes bright and candid. Dawn wanted to hide from them. Yet she found herself staring, paralyzed.

"Don't look so worried." Grace's fingers stroked Dawn's cheek, gently, then cupped her chin. Leaning closer, she brushed Dawn's mouth with her own, so lightly Dawn barely had time to register the touch.

By the time they were halfway back to the cottage, however, her face was burning and an oily nausea had invaded her stomach. Grace Ramsay had kissed her. On the mouth. No matter how convincingly she told herself that this was just an American way of being friendly, she couldn't forget the frankness in Grace's eyes.

Scared suddenly, she wished she could run far, far away — from the island, from Grace Ramsay, and from her own deafening heartbeat.

CHAPTER SEVEN

"Dawn! It's me, Cody." Footsteps halted on the veranda outside her bedroom window.

Dawn dragged herself out of bed, pulled on a sarong, and padded out, blinking in the buttercup light of morning.

Cody was standing on her veranda in a bedraggled straw hat and ancient cut-off jeans. "Fancy a spot of fishing?" she said.

"Fishing?" Dawn wrinkled her nose and considered the prospect of chopping up bait, gaffing fish and watching their tails thrash as life departed. She began to shake her head.

Cody eyed her knowingly. "I'll do all the nasty stuff. You can just sit there and hold on to a rod."

"Won't I be in the way?"

"Of course not. You'll balance the boat."

"Thanks a million. Now I feel really wanted."

Cody grinned at her. "Bring plenty of sun block. It gets hot out there."

She wasn't kidding. Cody's boat was a sixteen-foot runabout with a Mercury outboard. Its shallow canopy offered some protection from the endless sun, but after a couple of hours, Dawn's T-shirt was wet with sweat and her arms and legs were slick beneath the sun block she'd plastered on. They hadn't had a single bite.

Dawn adjusted her hat so the brim shadowed her neck more effectively. "They know it's me," she said crossly. "They know I hate catching them."

"You're talking about our dinner," Cody said. "I can't go home empty-handed. Annabel will kill me."

She said it so easily, so naturally, Dawn found herself staring. "Cody," she began in a thin little voice. "How did you know you were a . . . lesbian?"

Cody lowered her rod, a bemused expression on her face. "Why do you ask?"

Dawn was glad she was wearing sunglasses. "I just wondered. I'm sorry. You don't have to answer. I realize it's none of my business."

Cody shrugged. "I don't mind." Readjusting her

rod, she looked out at the hazy ocean. "It was a very long time ago, and it wasn't exactly a lightning bolt. I guess I knew I was a lesbian before I ever heard the word."

"What do you mean?"

"I've always had feelings for women, even as a kid. I always had a crush on someone."

"But that's normal, isn't it?" Dawn said, "I mean phases — they're a part of development."

"Well, there are two schools of thought on that. A lot of people believe we have no way of knowing what is *normal* until we stop pressuring young people so hard to be heterosexual."

"I don't feel pressured," Dawn objected.

"I see," Cody said blandly. "So you think it's perfectly okay for people to be gay? If you woke up tomorrow morning and saw *lesbian* printed on your forehead, you'd feel fine about walking downtown."

"Of course not," Dawn retorted.

"But you don't think that constitutes pressure?"

Looking at it that way, it was pressure, Dawn supposed. But then, being homosexual *wasn't* normal. In some places it wasn't even legal.

"Have you ever noticed that some people really hate gays?" Cody persisted. "Don't you think some of us might feel like we have a disease and maybe we should start going out with the opposite sex so people won't notice?"

Dawn changed hands on her rod, wiping one wet palm on her shorts. "Is that what you did?" she asked huskily.

"For a while," Cody admitted. "But I was lucky, I

guess. I ended up dating boys who were a bit like me. Safe company ..."

"Then you just started dating girls?"

"I guess you could say that. I fell in love a lot before I went into a relationship."

"Have you had a lot of ... relationships?" Dawn felt herself blush.

"Dawn!" Cody said with a laugh. "I think we've taken show and tell far enough for one day."

"I'm sorry, I didn't mean it like that. I meant ... Cody," she blurted. "Do you hate men?"

Cody laughed, a deep warm laugh. "Hate men? I'm not really interested enough in men to hate them."

Her comment startled Dawn; it echoed her own feelings so closely. Flustered, she adjusted the tension on her line and wiggled the hook experimentally. "But have you ever ... um."

"Have I ever had a relationship with a man? No, in a word."

"Then how do you know you're a lesbian?"

"How do you know you're straight?" Cody fired back. "Have you ever slept with a woman?"

Dawn blushed even more. She didn't want to think about yesterday, about Grace Ramsay. Besides, what had happened? A simple friendly little kiss. That was all. She squirmed in her seat. "It doesn't matter which way you look at it, Cody. We've got two sexes, right. Male and female. And nature attracts them to each other so that the human race continues. If everyone was homosexual, there'd be no more babies."

73

"I think you're mixing procreation with recreation. Do you only want sex when you're planning on having a baby?"

Dawn looked away. "Sex isn't that great," she muttered. "I can take it or leave it."

"I can't," Cody said flatly, and Dawn's mouth parted with shock.

Suddenly she found herself imagining it was Cody yesterday, not Grace. Horrified, she hunched her shoulders and stared morosely at her feet. How could she even think that for a second?

"Sex is wonderful," Cody was saying pointedly. "Especially when you're in love."

Dawn couldn't look up. She felt cornered, confused. She wasn't in love with Nigel. She'd never been in love with anyone. What was love, anyway? A racing heart, the sun setting on a tropical beach, violins playing. Was it sex on car seats, an engagement ring people stared at? She couldn't begin to imagine having the kind of feelings Cody was talking about. Maybe that was why sex had never interested her that much. She thought about Grace Ramsay again and suddenly she wondered what would have happened if she had returned that kiss.

Swinging her gaze back to Cody, she asked clumsily, "What do lesbians do —" Her line gave a sharp wrench, and she clutched her rod, shouting, "I've got one. I've got one."

She staggered to her feet only to be pushed straight back down onto the padded bench. Cody was beside her, locking the rod into the grips and adjusting the reel.

"Let it go," she said as the line screamed from the rod, yard after yard. "It's a biggie."

She secured a makeshift safety belt around Dawn's waist then scampered down to the stern, starting the outboard and hurling instructions at Dawn. The minutes ticked by, Dawn winding and winding, the boat dragging its anchor. The fish stayed on. Gradually, inch by inch it drew closer, then hurtled off toward the open sea again.

"I don't believe this," Cody said after it had made what felt like its thousandth bid for freedom.

"My arms are going to fall off," Dawn wailed. "It feels like we've got bloody *Jaws* on there."

Cody grinned, but there was a seriousness in the set of her mouth. "Maybe we have. I'll take over, if you like."

"No! I'm perfectly capable of catching a goddamn fish by myself." Dawn started winding anew, sweating and grunting, swearing under her breath.

Cody looked at her watch. "It's been on more than an hour."

Dawn traced the line out. The water sparkled bright turquoise. She was certain she'd caught a glimpse of something beneath the surface. "Look!" she yelled. About twenty feet from the boat the sea exploded and a huge silver fish twisted into the air.

"Shit! " Cody gasped. "A marlin."

Dawn was panting with the strain of its weight on the line. "It's enormous."

"Roll on dinner." Cody rubbed her hands. "Keep on winding," she ordered.

"I am bloody winding." Dawn felt as if she'd been hauling on that reel forever. The line was unbearably heavy. Dawn's muscles were screaming in violent protest.

Cody clipped herself to the safety line at the

stern of the boat and perched there with a long spike in her hand. A silvery head rose from the water, swinging back and forth, a straining body gleamed in the sun.

Dawn looked down into a black sorrowful eye. "No!" she screamed as Cody lifted the gaffe high. "Please . . . don't kill it."

Cody stared at her, uncomprehending, then she lowered the gaffe, groped in the bag at her feet and produced a set of pliers. Suspended over the edge of the boat, fending off the fish's sword with the gaffe, she strained down and snapped the hook cleanly apart.

Seconds later a tail broke the surface of the water and the marlin vanished.

They both stared after it, Dawn releasing sharp exhausted pants, Cody quiet and stunned.

"No one's ever going to believe us," Cody finally said.

Dawn shrugged. "The fish knows."

Dawn woke to the sound of her name being called. Blinking, she propped herself on her elbows and cocked her head.

"Dawn!" Someone was knocking on her door.

Opening the window beside her bed, she peered out.

Grace Ramsay was standing on the veranda. "Oh hell." She looked embarrassed. "Did I wake you?"

"I think I overslept." Yawning, Dawn glanced at

the clock on her dressing table. Midday! She'd slept for nearly eighteen hours. And it was the best sleep she'd had in months — since the accident, in fact.

"I'll come back later," Grace volunteered.

"No," Dawn said quickly. "It's okay. I'll get up now." Lowering her feet to the floor, she gathered up a sarong, wrapped it around herself and reached automatically for her pills. She twisted the cap then hesitated. Her legs felt surprisingly strong, the usual aching less pronounced. Hardly daring to believe her good fortune, she replaced the pill bottle and went to open the French doors.

Grace was reclining on the sunny wooden steps, her T-shirt damply outlining her breasts and shoulders. "I saw you out there yesterday," she said as Dawn emerged. "Shame you lost that fish. You did really well holding on so long." Her eyes were concealed behind dark lenses. "I was impressed."

Her throat looked very soft. A tiny dark mole nestled in the shadow of her left collarbone. Dawn experienced an odd desire to touch it. Feeling self-conscious, she blurted, "I don't much like fishing. It seems cruel."

"Then you're not sorry you lost the fish after all?" Grace's voice was faintly teasing.

"It never did me any harm. Why kill it?"

Grace removed her sunglasses. "Now don't tell me you collect for Greenpeace, Dawn." Her voice held a trace of cynicism.

"What's wrong with Greenpeace? At least they're doing something to stop us wrecking this planet." Dawn stopped, conscious of a sudden edge of discomfort about her visitor. What was Grace doing here anyway? Had she simply come over to pass the time of day, talking about fishing?

Straightening, she said, "Well, I'm going to take a shower. Is there something you wanted?"

"Do you have plans for the afternoon?" Grace inquired.

Dawn's heart sank. Clearly Grace was about to offer some kind of invitation. Remembering the awkward picnic, she said, "I've got some letters to write, and I thought I'd do some reading . . ."

Grace sought out her eyes. "So, is anyone cooking you dinner?"

Dawn felt color drift into her cheeks. Avoiding Grace's gaze, she tried to decipher the motivation behind these overtures of friendship. Perhaps Grace was simply a social kind of person, or maybe she was bored, stuck out here on an island when she was obviously used to a huge city. Or maybe she just felt sorry for Dawn.

Grace appeared to draw her own conclusions from Dawn's silence. With a casual shrug, she said, "Okay, so maybe you don't feel like company right now. I'll be home later if you change your mind. Just come on over." She started down the steps, then paused. "I'd like to see you," she added softly.

The dinner invitation plagued Dawn throughout the afternoon. Lying on the beach, her discarded Jackie Collins sticky with tanning lotion, she wondered why on earth Grace would want to spend time with her. She was certain Grace had no idea of her athletic fame back in Australia, and it wasn't as if they had anything in common apart from occupying neighboring cottages.

Her mind drifted to the picnic, to the way Grace had stared at her, and that one tiny kiss. Perhaps she was being paranoid about it, attributing ridiculous significance to what was merely a meaningless social gesture. On the other hand, Dawn strongly suspected Grace was a lesbian. And what if she were? Did that change anything?

Yes, it did, she conceded miserably. Fanning herself with her hat, she recalled her conversation on the boat with Cody. She was prejudiced, she realized. She was one of those people who laughed at gay jokes and made gay people feel bad about themselves. She had taken a dislike to Grace Ramsay for no other reason than she'd put together all the evidence that Grace was a lesbian. Ashamed of herself, she gathered up her possessions and started back to Frangipani Cottage.

The sun was sinking low in the sky and already the sounds of evening had started. It would be dark in a couple hours. She would light the lamps in her cottage and sit alone, probably feeling sorry for herself and wondering what to do with her life. And when there seemed no point in sitting up any longer she would shower, take her pills, and go to bed wondering what was really the point of it all.

Impulsively, she opened her wardrobe and pulled out one of the more appealing sundresses Trish had insisted she pack. Somehow she hadn't been able to bring herself to wear it yet. It seemed too bright with its yellow background and big red flowers. Dawn showered, put it on and studied herself critically.

The dress was close-fitting and short — too short perhaps. Staring at her thighs, Dawn fingered the scarred flesh. At least she'd tanned a little since she'd been on the island, and her muscles had regained some of their tone. Maybe she looked all right after all. Frowning, she brushed out her hair and put on a little lip gloss, leaving the rest of her face bare of makeup. Anyway, it didn't matter what she looked like. She was only having dinner with a woman.

Dabbing her wrists with Oscar de La Renta, she wrapped a few painkillers in a tissue, slid them into her pocket, and glanced in the mirror again. She could have been looking at her old self, she thought with a flash of pleasure. If it weren't for her legs, and ... there was something about her face too. Dawn studied her image, unable to figure out what was different. It was her eyebrows, she finally concluded. She hadn't plucked them in months.

"Tough," she said aloud. Facial torture — who needed it?

CHAPTER EIGHT

"You look great." Grace greeted her with a candid smile. "I was hoping you'd change your mind. I'd have a hell of a lot to eat if you hadn't." Leading Dawn into the sitting room, she said, "Make yourself comfortable. Can I get you a drink?"

Dawn asked for fruit juice. Alcohol didn't combine well with painkillers. She felt slightly disconcerted at the way Grace had set her table. It was very simple, but there were freshly picked flowers and candles. It looked ... romantic. To disguise her sudden nervousness, Dawn inquired, "How is your work going?"

"I'm pleased so far." Grace handed her a tall glass and joined her on the sofa. "I have a report to finish in the next few days, then maybe I'll get some time to play."

"What do you like to do . . . for play?"

"I like to get physical." She paused very deliberately, then added, "Squash, skiing, swimming. How about you?"

"I like swimming . . ." Even as she said it, her mouth started to tremble.

Grace looked a little awkward. "Are you okay?"

Dawn nodded. She didn't trust herself to speak.

"Hell, I'm sorry." Grace twisted her earring. "Touchy subject, huh?" She stood, extending a hand to Dawn. "Let's eat."

The meal was delicious: fish marinated in coconut milk, steamed rice and salad, followed by fresh mango and pawpaw.

"I'll miss the food here when I go home," Grace remarked as she served coffee. "It's so fresh. Mangos for breakfast, pineapples on the ground . . ."

"I'll miss the peace," Dawn said.

"It's quite a culture shock after the city, isn't it? What line of work are you in?"

Dawn sipped her coffee. "I'm trained as a kindergarten teacher."

Apparently, Grace noticed her lackluster tone. "A kindergarten teacher? Well, I'm surprised. You don't seem the little-kids type."

Dawn grimaced. "I'm not. I sort of had to do it." She fell silent, trying to figure out a way of changing the subject. She'd had a swimming scholarship, and it was a toss between the evils of accounting, teaching, or kindergarten. But her aborted career was not something she felt like discussing right now. "How about you? Did you always want to be a scientist?"

Grace cupped her chin. "Well, when I was a kid I had these grandiose fantasies about making some earth-shattering discovery and getting a Nobel Prize. I guess I took it from there."

"Do you think you might? Make a famous discovery, I mean." Dawn was slightly awestruck. Despite their previous conversation, she felt none the wiser about what Grace actually did. The woman was probably some kind of genius.

Grace was laughing, but her expression was cynical. "Hell no," she said. "I live in the real world now. Research science is all very glamorous, but the pay isn't. And besides, women are never credited for what we achieve. Look at DNA. Did Rosalind Franklin get the Nobel Prize? No, the boys did. I'm damned if I'm going to work my ass off so some man can get his name in the journals."

"You know, that's exactly what happens in sports too," Dawn said. "Some bloke gets into a final and he's a hero. A woman wins and she gets a couple of lines on the back page. It's not fair."

"Life's like that. The way I figure it, once you know the rules, you've got two choices — play to win, or don't play at all." Grace lifted the coffee pot. "More?"

Checking the time, Dawn declined. "I'll be up all night . . ."

"And you've got a tough day ahead of you, huh?" Grace's eyes were bold and teasing. "All that sunbathing and reading . . ."

Dawn smiled wryly. Her old training habits had certainly died hard. Early nights, up at five-thirty to swim for three hours before breakfast. She would never have to drag herself through that again. It was something to be grateful for, she supposed. "I'd better get going," she said. "It's late."

Grace was studying her. "Now there you go, looking sad again. I'd like to flatter myself that you're disappointed to be leaving so soon, but I guess not." She grinned suddenly, coaxingly. "You could stay and tell me about it over breakfast."

Dawn stiffened. What did that mean? She gazed uncertainly at the woman beside her, noticing the watchful intensity of her regard, the faint slow curving of her mouth. "No," she said hastily. "Er . . . thank you, anyway. I can find my own way back. I mean, you don't have to walk me."

Grace was all nonchalance. "Of course I'll walk you, Dawn." She offered her hand. "Shall we go, then?"

The velvet night air was warm and redolent with a mix of fragrances, the heady florals now so familiar to Dawn, and a spicier scent she recognized as Grace's. Following her closely along the narrow path to Frangipani Cottage, Dawn felt oddly chagrined. It was irrational, she thought, niggled by the feeling.

As they entered a small clearing a few minutes

away from the cottage, Grace paused, turning to place an arresting hand on Dawn's arm. "Do you smell that?" she murmured.

Inhaling deeply, Dawn became conscious of a powerful scent drifting across their path. "What is it?" she whispered.

"I'd swear it's Night Queen. That's a very rare lily that supposedly takes a hundred years to flower. You can only smell it at night."

"Wow." Dawn breathed. "It's incredible. It's like violets and vanilla ice cream . . ."

Grace was glancing around. "I wish I could find the plant. I noticed it a couple of nights ago and I looked for it the next morning. But without the scent to go by, it's virtually impossible to locate."

Dawn was impressed. A plant that released its fragrance only under cover of darkness. What a remarkable theft deterrent. Nature was smart that way. "Imagine owning one," she marveled. "You could die and never know what the flower looked like."

Grace smiled. "The perfect gift for the masochist who has everything." She pushed a stray curl off Dawn's forehead, fingers drifting out of contact then returning to linger for a moment on Dawn's hair. Her face was all shadows, her eyes brilliant black in the moonlight.

Staring up at her, Dawn felt transfixed, unwilling to move, to speak, to disturb in any way the fragile synthesis of that moment. They seemed enveloped by some profound silence, a lull in the deliberations of nature. They drew closer, bodies barely touching. Their mouths brushed lightly once, then again slowly and very thoroughly.

Dawn began to tremble. She was conscious of her

mouth parting, her eyes closing, her body tilting toward Grace's. The flat of Grace's hand burned where it rested against her back. Her mouth felt warm and soft and delicious. Dawn returned her kisses, timidly at first, then chaotically. She was aware of her dress being unzipped, of Grace's flesh meeting hers, of a confusion of scents — sweat, green jungle, the hint of cloves.

Responding to the coaxing pressure of Grace's tongue, she moved her mouth more urgently, shivering when Grace's hands began a purposeful exploration of her body. The sensations were unbearable, a trail of tiny explosions beneath her skin. Dawn's nipples were sore and wrinkled, exquisitely sensitive. Grace was sucking them, teeth softly tugging. "You like this?" she whispered as they sank onto the soft grass.

They rolled hard against each other, thighs locking. Twisting her fingers into Dawn's hair, Grace held her still for a moment, their faces close, breath merging. Then she was caressing Dawn's back and hips. Blood pounded in Dawn's ears as she felt her thighs nudged apart.

"Mmm . . . you're so slippery." Grace sighed.

Dawn's eyes flew open. Grace was touching her there where it was so wet and melting. "No!" She reached down, tearing the hand away. "Stop . . ."

"What is it?" Grace murmured against her mouth.

Dawn struggled, heat flooding her face. Clamping her thighs together, she jerked her head to the side, deeply ashamed. What in God's name was she doing, letting a woman touch her like that, encouraging her. She must be mad.

"Was it something I did?" Grace sounded

perplexed. "Am I going too fast for you?" She reached for Dawn, freezing when she was pushed away.

"Don't touch me!" Dawn cried.

"I don't understand. I thought you wanted this . . ."

Tears of humiliation stung Dawn's eyes. "Well, you were wrong."

"Dawn, how can you say that?" Grace shook her head, frustration entering her tone. "You're incredibly aroused. Please, tell me what's wrong? Is it your legs?"

"No! It's not my legs!" Dawn scrambled to her feet, dragging her dress over her shoulders. "There's nothing wrong with *me!* At least I'm normal."

Grace's gaze was black and piercing. "Let me get something clear," she said in a strained voice. "Are you a lesbian, Dawn?"

"Of course I'm not!" Dawn hurled at her.

"Oh, my God. I don't believe this." Laughing mirthlessly, Grace set about buttoning her shirt. "Kid," she addressed Dawn with deep irony. "If you're straight, I'm from Mars."

"Shut up!" Dawn shouted, backing away. "How could you do those disgusting things to me, then act like I'm the one with the problem!"

"You enjoyed those disgusting things," Grace yelled. "And if you weren't so damned hung-up, you'd have enjoyed a whole lot more of them."

"That's a filthy *lie.*" Dawn covered her ears. "I hated it and I hate you too."

"Fine," said Grace. "After that little episode the feeling's quite mutual. C'mon. I'll walk you home." Shoulders very stiff, she strode off into the jungle, calling carelessly, "Are you coming?" She paused then, laughing harshly. "No, of course you're not. It would be too much like having a good time, wouldn't it?"

"Shut up, you . . . you bitch!" Dawn felt like punching her. "I can find my own way back. I don't need you."

Grace turned, hands on hips. She said icily, "I wouldn't bank on that, sweetheart."

Perched on the edge of her bed after her shower, Dawn rubbed antiseptic cream into a long shallow scratch along one thigh. The injury had happened when she was stumbling home through the jungle. It was all *her* fault. Grace Ramsey's. She thought about those hands touching her, the feel of that body heavy and warm, that mouth. How dared she do that? What sort of woman was she?

A lesbian. That's what sort. A woman who . . . Dawn could hardly bear to contemplate it. Clutching her throbbing temples, she tried desperately to think of anything but Grace Ramsay. She felt hot and uncomfortable, her body unbearably tense. How could she have let that happen? One minute they were talking like civilized people, and the next minute they were kissing. Two women. It hardly seemed real.

Stuffing her hands between her legs, where she was still throbbing, she tumbled back onto her cool sheets. She'd had a lucky escape, she told herself. It could have been worse. At least Grace had stopped when she said no. She remembered a date she'd gone on once. It had been terrible, frightening. When she told her friends they just shrugged. It was normal . . . he was drunk. Next time don't let him in the house. Next time! Dawn shuddered, rejecting the image.

In the void, she could feel Grace's mouth, her skin, hear the bewilderment in her voice. Grace had thought she was a lesbian. How could she? Dawn didn't look anything like a lesbian. For an uncomfortable moment, she thought about Cody and Annabel, about Grace herself. They were exceptions, she decided. Any of them could get a man if she wanted to. But it looked like none of them did.

Why? Maybe something awful had happened to them when they were young, something that had turned them against men forever. Maybe they had been molested. How terrible. Well, that hadn't happened to her. She didn't hate men. She spared a moment's thought for Nigel. No, she didn't even hate Nigel. She just felt . . . nothing. It was all she'd ever felt, she thought guiltily. Even sex was . . . She groped for an adequate description. Tolerable . . . predictable . . . quick. Normal, in other words.

If there were women who had fantastic sex, she didn't know any of them. It happened in paperbacks, not real life. In real life it was all a bit of a letdown. *Give me a cigarette any day,* Trish always said. *It tastes better. Feels better. Lasts longer and you don't have to feed it.*

Disgusting, but true. Only . . . Dawn writhed miserably. She had never experienced anything like this. She hadn't known such sensations existed. It was mortifying. Of course there was a logical explanation. She had suffered a trauma. She wasn't herself. And she was on drugs. They'd obviously affected her behavior. She wasn't in full possession of her faculties.

None of this was her fault. She hadn't done anything to encourage Grace Ramsay. Quite the opposite, in fact. It was Grace who had pestered her, Grace who had obviously planned the whole thing, Grace who kissed her first.

She chewed her lip, wincing at the sweet salty taste of blood. Damn Grace Ramsay! If she never saw the wretched woman again, it would be too soon.

Cursing Dawn Beaumont under her breath, Grace slammed her cottage door, strode into the kitchen and hauled a bottle of Cognac out of the pantry. *Straight,* for God's sake. And broadcasting double messages every time she blinked those baby blue eyes.

For a moment Grace wondered if she'd been had. Maybe Dawn was playing games. Maybe this was how she got her kicks. Fooling around with lesbians then backing off quick when she couldn't take the heat.

Grace was appalled at herself. How could she have misjudged the situation so badly? Why hadn't she taken her time, played it cool? She'd been so sure Dawn would just fall into her bed, she'd blown it. What an amateur.

She poured a double and edgily prowled her sitting room. Being turned down so dramatically was something of a novelty. But who needed it? She pictured Dawn willing and responsive in her arms. The woman had wanted her. Damn it, she was just about coming before Grace had time to get her panties off.

Draining her glass, Grace licked the residue from her lips and gazed out her window. It was time she went home and got laid. She conjured up a vision of herself cruising babes at the Clit Club.

Dawn was too damned young, she decided. And implausible as it seemed, maybe she was just a straight woman who'd come down in the last shower of rain. Grace shook her head slowly. No. Dawn wasn't straight. Grace had played around with straight women. They were curious, titillated at their own daring, thinking they were doing you some kind of favor.

There was nothing furtive about Dawn's kisses, her body's clear signals. She just seemed . . . inexperienced. Grace toyed with the word and realized it fit perfectly. It had been so long since she'd had sex with a novice, she'd almost forgotten the classic symptoms. She recalled Dawn's tentative hands, her mouth frozen at first then responsive, her startled backing off. And suddenly she knew Dawn had never had sex with a woman before. She didn't even know she was a lesbian!

Grace almost laughed out loud. This put a whole new complexion on the situation. The Vuitton trunk wasn't such a lost cause after all. Strolling outdoors again, she peered into the dark mass of the jungle until she could just make out Dawn's cottage.

She could see her as clearly as day, tossing

miserably on her bed, wet and unfulfilled. Poor uptight little Dawn. She probably thought there was a law against masturbation too.

CHAPTER NINE

Robert B. Hausmann was the picture of geniality. He rose, offered his hand and pulled out a chair with studied ease, then settled comfortably back into his own chair.

Annabel seated herself and declined a drink. "I don't think this will take long," she said, removing the Argus folder from her satchel and extending it to her companion. "I've read this, Mr. Hausmann, and I'd like to thank you for the offer. But the answer is still no."

Robert Hausmann accepted the folder without a

blink. "I confess I'm disappointed, Annabel. I had hoped we might do business, but . . ." He shrugged, steepling his hands. "It's your decision, of course."

That was it? Annabel eyed him with suspicion. She had expected dismay at the very least. "I imagine you have other options," she angled.

"It's a big world out there . . . and with the changes in Europe . . . Well I'm the kind of guy who sees every setback as an opportunity."

"So you may not proceed with your plans for the South Pacific, after all?"

"Now, Annabel," he chided silkily. "You and I both know what that kind of inside information is worth on the open market."

It was obvious what Hausmann was getting at, Annabel thought. Once news of Argus's plans became public property, stock prices for its Pacific subsidiary would hit the roof. Anyone who had invested immediately prior would make a killing.

Hausmann apparently suspected her of trying to assess the prospects, trying to measure the impact of her decision. She found herself wondering how much stock he'd acquired lately and whether it could be traced to him.

"There have already been rumors," Hausmann noted. "It's almost impossible to keep this kind of thing quiet, as you know. We climbed ten points overnight. Of course, it could be disastrous for any big player, and it seems someone is in the market right now . . ."

"A hostile takeover bid, perhaps?" Annabel speculated sweetly.

The barb went straight home, registering in the thinning of his mouth. "Nothing on that scale." He flicked a dismissive hand. "Between you and me, I've heard it's some bankrupt banana republic taking a flyer."

The words had a chilling deliberation about them. Surely the Cook Islands Premier wouldn't take a chance like that, Annabel thought. Not with government money. Hausmann had to be bluffing.

He was on his feet. "I'm sorry I can't spend more time in your charming company. I gather there's nothing I can offer that will persuade you to change your mind?" He added it almost as an afterthought.

"I have everything I want in life, Mr. Hausmann," Annabel responded coolly. "Selling Moon Island would be a loss, not a gain."

"Well, I'm sorry you feel that way. Very sorry. And I'm sure I won't be the only one." With a chill smile, he walked away, leaving Annabel gazing uneasily after him.

A short while later, as she was preparing to leave, a waiter approached and handed her an envelope, explaining that Mr. Hausmann had asked if she would deliver it to one of her guests.

With a jolt, Annabel read the name scrawled across it. Dr. Grace Ramsay.

Grace sagged back against a leafy papaya tree and disconsolately sipped from her flask. It was dusk and she had found no trace of the elusive Night Queen. By the time the first hint of that exotic fragrance wafted into the tropical night, the jungle would be enveloped in darkness, its most tightly held secrets safe once more from prying humanity.

She only hoped she could track the plant down before she left. It was a specimen any institution would be pathetically grateful for, exactly the kind of donation that would reap vast public relations gains for Argus. Envisaging tangible expressions of Robert Hausmann's gratitude, Grace methodically surveyed the area around her.

Tomorrow she would plan out a grid search, she decided. This would be her only chance to find the wretched plant. As soon as the island was sold, Argus would move in with chemical defoliants to make the place more accessible. Of course, it would not be as pleasant with dense greenery eliminated, but progress had its price.

Brushing twigs from her legs, Grace wondered whether Annabel Worth had signed on the dotted line yet. Five million dollars. Only a complete fool, or a sentimentalist, would turn down that kind of offer. The Annabel Worth Grace remembered was neither of those.

Grace marveled at the quirk of fate that had brought her to the very island Annabel owned. It had come as quite a shock to arrive in Rarotonga to find her one-time Boston fling waiting to escort her. If anything, Annabel was even more desirable than she had been six years ago. Something about her had mellowed to the point where it was almost impossible to reconcile the laid-back, sensual Annabel who flew the Moon Island shuttle with the brittle stockbroker who had once told Grace she found coffee more satisfying than sex.

Grace had briefly entertained the possibility of a renewed liaison. But Annabel had quickly made it clear that she was unavailable, and meeting Cody

Stanton, Grace could certainly see why. Annabel and her beloved were obviously joined at the hip, a veritable billboard for monogamous bliss. Doubtless a commitment ceremony would be the next milestone, then the search for a sperm donor ... Where would it end?

Grace reached the large stand of frangipani flanking Dawn's cottage and deliberated for a moment on the merits of dropping in. Maybe Dawn would buy an apology. *Forgive me. I was overcome. You looked so sweet and beautiful in the moonlight. For one magical moment it would have been easy to believe we were in love. I wanted just to kiss you, yet when I started I couldn't stop. You were so warm and willing ...*

No, the outraged young Australian wouldn't have a word of it, Grace guessed. Yet ironically, it was the truth. There had been something special about standing beneath the stars with Dawn, that unworldly scent drifting by, the tropical night laden with promise. Grace glanced at the cottage and gave a small cynical laugh. There must be something in the Moon Island breeze, she decided, something that softened the brain.

Dawn paced her veranda restlessly. Her thoughts were clattering like a toy train, returning again and again to that disastrous encounter with Grace. She wanted desperately to erase from her consciousness the pressure of Grace's mouth, the warmth of her hands, but the disturbing memories persisted. And far from gaining satisfaction at the triumph of her common sense over these new and inexplicable physical urges, Dawn felt oddly bereft.

She stared up at the moon. It was pale orange, full and alluring against the dark sky. Beyond the palms, the ocean glowed like a black pearl. It was the perfect night for a swim. The very idea made Dawn yearn for the satiny solace of water. Impulsively, she went indoors, gathered up a large towel, and pulled on some sandals.

A narrow track led through a musky entanglement of vines and leaves to the beach. Dawn tossed her stick, clothing and shoes into a pile on the sand and lay down beneath the starry tapestry of the sky. The beauty of the night was heart-stopping. It was so still — just the throbbing cadence of the ocean and the occasional sigh of the palms in response to an indecisive breeze.

Trickling sand through her fingers, Dawn thought about the fish she had released. It was out there somewhere in the milky ocean, swimming and swimming. She almost wished she could trade places with it. Rolling onto her stomach, she propped her chin on her forearms and stared out to sea.

A dark blob on the ocean's surface drew her attention. It was moving slowly across the bay. She caught a glimpse of arms and froze. A swimmer. Some other person in her bay, intruding on her night. Grace Ramsay. Who else could it be? The blob drew closer to the beach. It loomed out of the water, stretched languidly, then shook its head.

Closing her eyes, Dawn tried to block out the sight of that body, lithe and naked, glistening in the moonlight. Grace paused, staring along the beach as though she could sense someone's presence. Dawn held her breath, kept her head low, willed herself not to move a muscle. But when Grace started walking, panic mobilized her limbs and, scrambling to her feet, she lurched toward the jungle.

"Dawn! It's you." The voice was shockingly near. "Come on in. The water's incredible."

Dawn's stomach curled. Her legs were suddenly heavy and irresolute. She glanced back over her shoulder. "I didn't mean to disturb you," she said in a voice that barely sounded like her own. "I didn't know anyone was here."

Grace halted only when she was so close their bodies were nearly touching. In the moonlight, droplets of water studded her skin like thousands of tiny jewels. "I'm glad you're here," she said. Her voice was very soft, no suggestion of her former anger.

Dawn wished she could read her expression. There was just a smile, white in the darkness of her face.

"Come on." Grace reached casually for her hand. "I won't bite."

Vacillating, Dawn glanced toward the beckoning sea. She wished she could feel angry at Grace, walk away from her, proud and defiant. But instead she allowed herself to be led across the sand.

"Wonderful night, isn't it?" Grace said as they waded into the sea.

Dawn croaked a meaningless response. She was glad of the darkness so her burning cheeks wouldn't show. Lapping around her thighs, the water was warm, infinitely soothing. She sank into it, weightless, relieved of the aching pressure of standing, and swam a slow arc around the bay.

She would have her swim and then go home, Dawn resolved. There was no need to be frightened of Grace. The whole thing had been a mistake. Grace probably wanted to forget it as much as she did. Reaching the shallows, she got to her feet. There was no sign of Grace in the moonlit waters, no seal-like head bobbing, no splash of feet.

Dawn stared around, calling, "Grace. Where are you?" She flinched as the surface broke directly in front of her.

"I'm right here."

"You scared me."

"I seem to be making a habit of that."

"Let's just forget about it . . . what happened, I mean."

"If that's what you want. I've found it hard thinking about anything else."

Dawn tucked her hands into her armpits to stop them shaking. She didn't want to have this conversation. "I'm sorry if I gave you the wrong impression," she mumbled.

"I don't think you did." With slow deliberation, Grace touched Dawn's shoulder, her thumb brushing the hollow at the base of her neck. "We could start again," she said. "Would you like that?"

Dawn's first urge was to back away, but her feet seemed embedded in the sand. She felt as though she were sinking, drowning. The crashing of her heart was louder than the distant waves against the reef. Suddenly she knew she wanted what Grace was offering. Wanted it more than she'd ever wanted anything. But she didn't know what to do. "I can't . . ." she began.

Drawing closer, Grace lowered her mouth to the base of Dawn's throat, her tongue trailing slowly downward to capture the salty rivulets converging between her breasts. "We can pretend we just met," she said softly. "But by some magic we know each other well." She took Dawn's face between her hands, kissing her delicately, on the hair, the eyelids, the cheeks. "Don't be scared," she murmured. "I know this is new for you."

Dawn took a shaky breath. Her senses were clamoring, her lips full and craving. She could feel Grace's breath on her face, feel her own moisture trickling down her thighs to merge with the salt water.

"Just for tonight," Grace whispered against her lips, and this time Dawn's mouth parted and her outstretched fingers met Grace's flesh. Trembling, she moved closer, aware of their breasts sliding across one another, nipples as hard as little pebbles. Grace's mouth was on her neck, then her shoulders. Their stomachs brushed, then Grace was holding her hips and Dawn felt the new and shocking sensation of another woman's sex pressed into hers.

She stiffened for a split second, then Grace's arms gathered her close. Suddenly she felt safe. Taking Grace's hand, she allowed herself to be guided slowly out of the water. They stood in each others' arms, returning kiss for kiss. Dawn stroked her fingers along Grace's spine, awed by the texture of her flesh, the firm outline of her muscles. She rested her hands in the small of Grace's back then moved on to the wonderful roundness of her bottom.

Then there was sand beneath her head, Grace's

breasts crushed to hers, their thighs entwined. Gentle surf fingered its way up the sand to bubble and lap across their legs.

Leaning over her, Grace was breathing hard. "Do you want me?" she demanded huskily.

Trapped in the intensity of her gaze, Dawn struggled to find the words. "I don't know what to do," she whispered.

Grace's arms closed around her. "Yes you do."

And she was lifted into the air, Grace's mouth on hers, warm and intoxicating. Moments later she was lying on something soft. Her towel. Grace was caressing her, long sensual strokes which extended from her breasts to the parting of her thighs. Unbearable heat spread through her pelvis. Parting her legs, she placed her hands on Grace's shoulders. "I want you," she said.

Grace moved over her, blotting out the moon, erasing the pulse of the ocean, the green jungle smell, until Dawn could feel only her, smell only her. She shivered as Grace slid an arm beneath her hips, trailed warm kisses across her stomach and over her thighs and finally found the ache between them. Centered where they were most exquisite, the sensations multiplied until Dawn's whole body was rising and falling, fiercely concentrated on this sensual rite. Moisture broke across her skin. She clung to Grace, grounding herself in the feel and smell of her.

Then she was crying, rocked against the safety of Grace's shoulder, Grace's soft voice repeating, "It's all right, baby. It's all right."

CHAPTER TEN

When Dawn awoke, she was alone. The clock beside Grace's bed said noon.

She had slept for hours, a deep, satisfying sleep. Eyes closed, she recaptured for a moment the sensations of the night, then stretched languidly and pushed back the sheets, bathing in the breeze that seeped through the window.

Somewhere on the outer reaches of her consciousness, she could make out the sounds of another person moving about in the cottage, footfalls, the occasional thud or clatter. A hot-water kettle whistled; a woman was humming. On a hook behind Grace's door were a couple of brightly colored sarongs. Knotting one of these to cover her breasts, Dawn pushed her tangled hair off her face and ventured out in the direction of the noises.

Grace was at the small table in the kitchen, pouring a cup of tea. As Dawn hovered in the doorway, Grace glanced up, smiling broadly. Dawn flushed. She didn't want to, but the sight of Grace in her white shirt and khaki shorts, her eyes dark and knowing, made her feel exposed. What must Grace think of her, she wondered.

"Sleep well?" Grace asked. She didn't seem embarrassed or jumpy.

Murmuring some inconsequential response, Dawn found herself fascinated by Grace's slender, purposeful hands as they poured tea, buttered a roll. She quickly lowered her head, certain her graphic memories of those hands were written all over her face.

"I was hoping you'd wake before I go," Grace said nonchalantly.

Dawn looked up. "Go? Where are you going?"

"I'm borrowing Cody's boat for the afternoon to do some depth-testing out near the reef."

"I see." Inching her way into the room, Dawn sat down at the table. Why did she feel so dejected all of a sudden? Grace was just carrying on life as usual. What had she expected? "When will you be back?" The words were out before she could prevent them and Dawn felt a rush of irritation at herself.

Grace shrugged. "It's hard to say." She wore a slightly guarded expression. "What are your plans for the day?"

"Nothing in particular."

"You could come with me if you want." The invitation sounded tentative.

She was offering out of politeness, Dawn decided, and quickly shook her head. "No . . . . no thanks. I'll give it a miss."

Grace's glance became intent. "Are you upset about last night, Dawn?"

Upset? Dawn struggled with the question. No, that didn't begin to describe how she was feeling. Devastated was more like it, stunned, overwhelmed. She felt as though she had stumbled into some kind of emotional maze and would never find her way back. Bemused, she shook her head.

Grace must have interpreted this as embarrassment, for she said, "We don't have to talk about it if you'd rather not. Last night never happened . . . okay?"

Dawn stared at the floor. Grace might be able to easily dismiss what they'd done, but she certainly couldn't.

"It doesn't worry me," Grace was assuring her, and this time Dawn detected a harder note. "I had a good time and I think you did too. Let's just leave it at that. No strings attached, okay?"

Dawn's throat felt swollen. "Okay," she croaked. *Liar!* her mind shouted. She wanted to get up, throw her arms around Grace, beg her not to go. She wanted them to lie naked in the truth of daylight and make love all over again. But Grace was getting to her feet, brushing off her shorts, glancing at her watch. Clearly this was just a morning like any other morning for her. Maybe she did this kind of thing all the time.

Dawn stood too, arms folded across her breasts. Hungry butterflies chewed a wayward path from the pit of her stomach to the cleft between her legs. "I'd better be going," she said in a high brittle voice. "I've got some letters to write."

Grace gave her another piercing look. "Dawn ..." she began, then seemed to reconsider, her mouth wry. "You don't have to rush off," she said in a neutral tone. "Help yourself to breakfast ..."

Averting her eyes, Dawn muttered a low thanks. Breakfast. Only minutes ago she had been starving but now the very thought of food made her nauseous.

Grace was suddenly so close their bodies were brushing. "Are you really okay, Dawn?"

Dawn was tempted then to spill out all her feelings, but something in Grace's eyes prevented her. There was an unmistakable reserve, a distancing that pulled her up short. Grace didn't really want to hear what she was feeling, Dawn realized with sharp dismay. Tongue-tied, she turned her attention toward the empty cups on the table and started gathering them up. "Nothing's wrong, Grace," she said, forcing indifference. "Have fun on the boat."

Meeting Grace's eyes, she caught a quick, shuttered glimpse of relief. Then Grace was twisting her earring, her face relaxing into a lopsided grin.

"Have fun with your letters," she said. And blowing Dawn a kiss, she sauntered from the room, apparently without a care in the world.

* * * * *

With a mixture of emotions, Annabel knocked on Grace's door-frame and waited. Six years had passed since they were lovers, and it had been a shock to see Grace after so long. She'd been on the island for nearly three weeks and Annabel had felt an occasional pang of guilt for keeping her distance.

She'd told Cody about Grace, emphasizing the fact that their relationship was never serious. They only saw each other when they happened to be visiting their respective cities on business. Their contact was composed of no more than a series of pleasant sexual encounters. Annabel knew Cody had difficulty understanding. She was such a straightforward person. Why have casual sex when you can have a full-time lover and genuine romance? It was as simple as that.

There was no answer from inside the cottage. Dropping into one of the cane veranda chairs, Annabel contemplated the gardens around her. It had been a massive job to reestablish them after Hurricane Mary, but now it was difficult to tell that this part of the island had been so badly ravaged.

The jungle was a fleshy tangle of leaves and vines. It hummed with late-afternoon activity, creatures heading for home. Annabel experienced the same powerful urge herself, imagining Cody on the veranda immersed in some paperback, herself pottering in the kitchen. Briefly she wallowed in private delight. She wouldn't swap this life for anything, least of all a bank balance and a pile of scrip.

Glancing at the envelope on the table in front of her, she wondered why Robert B. Hausmann was writing to Grace. What exactly had Grace said about her research work on the island? Something obscure to do with coral reef formations. Annabel hadn't paid much attention at the time. She was too busy trying to sort out her feelings about having a piece of her past return to haunt her.

Had Grace mentioned whom she was working for? No. Had she concealed it deliberately? Annabel frowned. Somewhere in the back of her mind a nasty little doubt hovered, reminding her that Grace was an opportunist from way back. She hadn't let ethics stand in her way in the past, and from the inviting look she'd given Annabel right under Cody's nose, that evidently hadn't changed.

"Annabel!" a voice hailed her.

Grace emerged from a thicket of vines. She looked surprised, pleased, and Annabel found her pulse responding to those dark assessing eyes.

"It's good to see you," Grace said. She paused, hands on hips, catching her breath.

Watching her breasts rise and fall, Annabel allowed herself to remember that body. She felt oddly detached. Grace Ramsay was one of the most exciting lovers she'd ever had. It was strange to see her now and feel nothing of the sexual pull that had first drawn them together. "I have something for you, Grace," she said. "From Robert Hausmann."

Grace looked briefly startled, then an untroubled calm descended on her features and she took the envelope, sliding it casually into her shorts pocket.

"You're acquainted with Mr. Hausmann?" Annabel asked.

Grace's eyes were calculating. Annabel could

almost hear her weighing up her options, trying to guess how much Annabel actually knew. "Don't even think about lying to me, Grace," she challenged coldly. "We know each other better than that."

For a moment there was a hint of chagrin in Grace's expression, then she shrugged. "I'm employed by Argus. I can't say I know Robert Hausmann personally. We've met, that's all."

"What are you doing here?"

"Some research."

"For Argus?"

"That's right."

"Did you know Argus wants to buy the island from me?"

Grace hesitated. "I gathered so. We need a base out here. Housing for staff . . . that kind of thing."

It sounded glib. "So you're here for three weeks to find out whether the island's habitable? Stretches credibility, Grace."

"That's not my problem. I'm just doing my job."

"I want to see your report," Annabel demanded.

Grace jerked upright. "No. Absolutely not. That report's confidential."

"As from today that report's totally irrelevant," Annabel tossed back. "I've turned down your boss's offer to buy the island."

Grace looked momentarily uncertain, then she said, "That doesn't make any difference. Argus commissioned a report and I'll deliver it. If you want to see it you'd better speak to Robert Hausmann."

Annabel took a deep breath. Grace was hiding something. Everything about her shouted it. She looked cagey, defensive. "Grace, please," Annabel pressed her. "What is Argus really doing out here? I can't swallow some line about office premises in the middle of nowhere."

Grace fell silent. Her eyes glinted with appreciation. "You know," she drawled, "being in love has done wonders for your sex appeal, Annabel."

"Grace! I'm asking you a question."

"Give me a break. You know I can't answer that."

"The word is *won't*, not can't. Look, Grace, this is my home. I have a right to know what some huge conglomerate is doing sniffing around here."

"You're asking me to be disloyal . . . to breach confidentiality."

"When was that ever a problem?"

"Don't pull that one on me, Annabel. You were no saint yourself. You were still with Claire when you went to bed with me."

"You know damned well Claire and I were breaking up. I was depressed and upset."

"You were horny."

Annabel took a sharp breath. "And you were still living with Carol."

"So what? She knew I saw other women."

"She knew you weren't capable of being committed, you mean!"

"I don't have to listen to this." Grace stalked into the cottage, Annabel marching after her. "I can't see why you're so damned obsessed with my report. You're not selling the island anyway, so what the hell does it matter to you?"

"I don't expect you to understand. You obviously don't give a damn about anybody except yourself. But we're not all like you." Annabel met Grace's eyes levelly. "I care about these islands and the people living here, and I want to know what Argus is up to. Don't worry," she added with deep cynicism. "I won't advertise it. Your ass will be covered."

Grace's gaze fell to the document sitting on the coffee table. Breathing hard, her mouth tight with anger, she snatched it up and thrust it at Annabel.

Annabel grabbed the report, sat down and began skimming the scientific text. After a few minutes, she lifted her head and said, "I can't believe you're involved in this."

Grace stared at her, hard-eyed. "What's the crime, Annabel?"

"You're talking about exploding half the reef around the island, about incinerating toxic chemicals and burying the waste. Razing the vegetation, destroying the habitats of every creature on the island." She was shaking. "This is sickening."

"Oh, for God's sake, Annabel. Where've you been all your life? We produce five hundred million tons of hazardous waste a year back home. The stuff has to be dumped somewhere."

Annabel cradled her head in her hands. If they didn't get Moon Island, they were bound to find an alternative. The Cook Islands would become another Marshalls, people dying slowly from the effects of windborne contamination. "Grace, how can you do this?" A sob was working its way into her throat. "How can you work for these people?"

"Argus is a responsible company," Grace said hotly. "They value my skills. What do you expect me to do? Martyr myself to some poverty-stricken, ecologically sound bunch of do-gooders . . ."

"I don't expect anything of you," Annabel said

bitterly. "I can't believe you stayed here doing this behind my back. How could you be so dishonest? We were lovers!"

"We were fucking," Grace hissed. "That's all. Spare me the guilt trip, for chrissakes. We can't all afford to wallow in high-blown ethics. Some of us have to work for a living. It so happens my career is important to me. In fact, it's the most important thing in the world."

Annabel felt a rush of sadness. The Grace she remembered hadn't been this hard. What on earth had happened to her in the past five years? "If that's true, then I can only feel sorry for you."

"Don't torture yourself," Grace retorted. "I'm perfectly happy."

"I'm going now." Annabel dropped the report disgustedly on the table. "I'd like you to leave the island. You can come with me to Rarotonga the day after tomorrow.

Grace shrugged. "Suits me. I've finished here anyway."

They stood side by side on the veranda for a long moment, gazing out at the amethyst twilight. Then Annabel said very quietly, "I'm sorry it's turned out like this, Grace." Turning, she caught a glimpse of pain in Grace's eyes and impulsively touched her arm, pleading, "Grace, what's happened to you?"

Grace's expression was glazed. "Is it that obvious?"

"I haven't forgotten absolutely everything about you," Annabel said in a dry tone. "Want to talk about it?"

Grace hesitated. She looked numb, as if dispossessed of her senses. "I don't know if I can," she said.

Annabel raised her hand to Grace's shoulder. "Maybe it's time you found out."

The sun was low and orange when Dawn decided she couldn't stand another moment of dithering around in Frangipani Cottage, obsessing over Grace Ramsay. Donning a light sweater and jeans, she hobbled resolutely into the jungle and along the narrow track to Grace's cottage.

Where was her pride, she thought unhappily. Wasn't it enough she'd gone to bed with a virtual stranger, without it being a woman and without going back for seconds? For that was what she was doing. She couldn't pretend she was seeking Grace out for intellectual stimulation or pleasant company on a long tropical night. No. She wanted her. The admission was so shocking that Dawn stopped in her tracks, the squashy nighttime sounds of the island providing a lurid backdrop to her thoughts. She was hot and throbbing between her legs, empty where she wanted to be full. She started walking again.

Creepers caught at her hair and her hands felt damp and sticky from grappling with the tangled vegetation. Darkness was falling swiftly, and for a moment she felt frightened she would never find her way out. Then she caught the sound of music, melodious but slightly tinny. Grace's battery operated cassette player.

An involuntary smile tugged at the corners of her

mouth. She would never be able to hear that particular Annie Lennox tape without remembering. But there was something else. Voices. She peered between the huge leaves of a papaya.

They were standing on the veranda, Grace and another woman she couldn't quite see. Dawn debated whether to go on. She told herself she was being stupid. Even if Grace did have a visitor, she wouldn't mind her showing up. But somehow it wasn't the same. She didn't want to arrive at Grace's cottage as an uninvited third party. That wasn't the mental picture she'd fabricated: Grace surprised and delighted to see her, the two of them melting into each other's arms.

Crestfallen, she contemplated the women on the veranda. She should never have come, she thought dismally. She was behaving like a lovesick adolescent. Her eyes stung and she balled her fists against them. How could this have happened to her? It was some kind of divine retribution, she decided, the inevitable consequences of tempting fate. It was her punishment for thinking the things she had about women like Cody and Annabel . . . lesbians.

Now she'd had an affair with one of them, even if it had only lasted a night. And here she was, the very next day, hanging out for more . . .

Numbly, she focused on the two women. They appeared to be deep in conversation, heads close together. Then she recognized Annabel Worth. Her arm was over Grace's shoulder and as Dawn watched they moved together, holding each other.

She jerked her head away. She couldn't bear to

114

see any more. Blindly, she stumbled back into the night. Grace and Annabel! She felt like throwing up. How could they?

CHAPTER ELEVEN

"Are you tired?" Cody bent over Annabel and planted a kiss on her forehead. Annabel had seemed oddly preoccupied ever since she got home from Rarotonga the day before.

"I'm sorry, darling. I'm not much company this morning, am I."

Sliding her arms loosely around her lover's neck, Cody nuzzled her cheek. "We could work on that."

Annabel stroked Cody's hair. "I love you," she murmured.

"I love you too." Cody observed Annabel's frown with a twinge of apprehension. "Is something wrong?"

Annabel hesitated. Then she said wearily, "Grace is working for Argus, the company trying to buy the island. She's been writing a report on how to turn Moon Island into a chemical dump."

Cody was aghast. "She never said a word! What a lousy . . ." She trailed off. You weren't supposed to call your lover's ex a rotten bitch.

Annabel looked wry. "It's okay, Cody. I've found this a low-wattage experience too."

"What are we going to do about it?"

"It's already done. I've told Hausmann we're not selling and I've asked Grace to leave. I'll be taking her with me tomorrow."

"Is that why you went to see her last night?"

Annabel nodded. "I gave her a pretty hard time. I guess I feel kind of lousy about it now."

"*You* feel lousy!" Cody snorted. "You're not the one who just accepted women's hospitality and snuck around behind their backs arranging to destroy their environment."

"She said she's sorry. Don't think too badly of her, Cody. Grace has had a few problems lately. I don't think they've enhanced her perspective."

Cody bit back a sharp comment. If Annabel wanted to defend her ex's disgusting behavior, that was up to her. It must be hard to admit you'd slept with such a jerk, even if it was only casual. She reached across and took Annabel's hand. "I'm just glad she's going and it's all over with these Argus people."

"I'm glad too," Annabel said.

Her voice was flat and controlled, but there was an edge of something else. Trying to ignore the shiver that crept along her spine, Cody kissed her softly. "It *is* over, isn't it?" she persisted.

Annabel gazed out the window. "I'm not sure. I guess I was expecting Hausmann to put up more of a fight. Back home he's got a reputation for getting his way."

"You mean he's ruthless?"

"He plays to win," Annabel said. "But this time he backed down like a lamb."

Cody shrugged. "Well, then. It's all over. He'll just have to find some other place to set up shop." She stroked Annabel's hair. "Don't worry about it, darling. No one's going to take the island away from us."

"Sometimes I get frightened," Annabel said in a muffled voice. "It all feels too good to be true ... that I have you and we live in this beautiful place. I'm scared that one day I'll wake up and find it was all a dream."

Drawing Annabel close, Cody kissed her passionately. "Did that feel real?"

Returning her kisses with an urgency that verged on desperation, Annabel whispered, "I love you, Cody." Taking Cody's shoulders, she drew back suddenly, eyes intense. "Promise me something," she said. "If anything ever happens to me, you won't give up the island."

"Annabel!" Cody shivered. "What are you talking about?"

"Just promise," Annabel insisted.

Cody stared at the woman she loved. "I promise," she said uneasily.

Dawn was on her veranda when Grace sauntered into view. The mere sight of her made her stomach lurch. She looked so relaxed and open, so fatally charming. And she was having an affair with Annabel Worth. They were ratting on Cody.

Climbing the steps, she offered Dawn an insolent half-smile. "God, I could use a drink," she said.

Dawn gave her a frosty look. "Help yourself. You know where the kitchen is."

Grace didn't seem to notice her chilly reception. Tossing her hat down beside her chair, she asked, "You want anything?"

Only to slap that grin off your face, Dawn thought. But she said, "No thanks." Grace returned with a large glass of pineapple juice and sat in the chair beside Dawn's. She stretched out her legs, kicking off her sandals with an easy familiarity that rattled Dawn more than she could believe. How dare she! How dare she come bowling in in all innocence when she was carrying on with some other woman who was already in a relationship.

Dawn didn't realize she was glaring until Grace tilted her head and those dark eyes flashed knowingly. "Are you mad at me, Dawn?"

"No. Why should I be?"

"Why indeed?" Grace sipped her drink, her gaze firmly riveted to Dawn's face. "Are you upset I didn't come over last night?"

"No doubt you had better things to do," Dawn said stonily.

"I get the feeling you're trying to tell me something. What is it?"

Dawn shrugged. She felt out of her depth. What right did she have to demand explanations from Grace about her behavior? They'd spent a night together. So what? Wiping her hands across her T-shirt, she tried not to notice the smooth length of Grace's thighs, the faint sharp smell of cloves. Her attention drifted to the parting of Grace's shirt, the press of those raisin-dark nipples, the shadow of her breasts.

She wanted to touch her. She wanted to lie with her naked, wallow again in that mindless pleasure. Self-disgust made her look away. How could she even consider it? What had she turned into, a slave to some previously unsuspected carnality? She reminded herself brutally that Grace was a liar and a home-wrecker. But her body cried, Who cares?

"I'm leaving the island tomorrow," Grace said quietly. "I've come to say goodbye."

"Goodbye?" Dawn repeated.

"I've finished my work." There was a newer harder note. "So I'm flying out with Annabel."

With Annabel. Dawn tried not to react.

"I just wanted to tell you." Grace fidgeted with her earring. "I enjoyed our time together."

This was it, Dawn thought bitterly. Thanks for the sex, sweetheart. See you later. Later as in never. Her fingers dug into her palms, making tight little fists. She felt like punching Grace in the teeth.

Instead she jerked to her feet and on the most offhand note she could muster, said, "Well I'll be seeing you then." Turning away from Grace, she stared out to sea. She would not cry in front of this woman. Grace Ramsay could rot in hell, as far as she was concerned.

"Dawn." A hand touched her shoulder. "We don't have to do it this way. You're angry at me and I don't even know why." Grace drew Dawn slowly around, sliding her arms loosely about Dawn's waist.

Dawn felt her eyes drawn inexorably to Grace's. She watched the pupils dilate, the thick straight lashes droop with sleepy sensuality. Her lips parted to frame a sentence telling Grace exactly what she thought of her, but the words never came. Instead something tangible and shockingly lusty passed between them, and Dawn lifted her fingers to Grace's mouth. It was soft, a little dry. She bent forward, moistened it with her tongue, felt it part invitingly.

The kiss deepened. Dawn twisted Grace's shirt roughly from her shorts. She couldn't stop shaking.

Grace laughed softly. "What's the rush?" Her hands moved to Dawn's buttocks, pressing her closer. Her eyes were full of wicked intent. "You want me, Dawn?"

A gush of liquid soaked Dawn's pants. Grace took one of her hands, kissed the scars across its knuckles then guided it between her own thighs, sliding it back and forth across the damp seam that parted her flesh. Her mouth on Dawn's neck, hot and insistent. Dawn increased the pressure of her fingers, irked at the fabric barrier that denied them their destination. She tugged at Grace's shorts and gasped as her nipples were pinched. Grace whispered in her ear, "So, what are you going to do about it then?"

Breathing hard, Dawn seized one of Grace's hands and pulled her toward the cottage. She wanted her so badly she felt sick. Once in her room she pushed Grace onto her bed and fell on top of her, tugging clumsily at her clothes. Grace laughed softly and took over, deftly removing the offending garments. Then she rolled Dawn onto her back, pinning her shoulders down.

"You'll have to wait," she murmured hoarsely. "I want you first." She slid first one knee, then the other, between Dawn's thighs and lowered herself over Dawn, kissing her passionately. As the strength fled Dawn's limbs, Grace's kisses subtly altered. Slowly, sensually, she moved her mouth over Dawn's cheek, to her ear.

She bit Dawn's neck softly, and again harder, watched the mark of her teeth blossom. Then she wound her fingers into Dawn's hair and for a sweet moment rested her cheek between her breasts. "Your heart is beating so fast," she whispered, drawing Dawn upright so that they were facing each other.

Dawn couldn't speak. She was frightened. Frightened at the degree of intimacy between them. She had never felt so completely exposed, so vulnerable. For a split second she wanted to stop, then Grace was holding her, cradling her, knowing her as no one ever had before.

* * * * *

Hours later, Dawn lay against Grace's shoulder and listened to the steady beat of her heart. She ran an exploring hand across Grace's small taut breasts, her flat stomach, the springy curls of her pubic hair. Then she did the same with herself, first the stomach, then the soft straight hair between her own legs, and her full heavy breasts.

Her body felt brand new, barely familiar, its contours redefined. Grace knew exactly how to touch her. She must have made love with dozens of women, Dawn thought with a pang. Probably beautiful, clever women who were fantastically accomplished in bed. Turning her face into Grace's breast, she stretched her tongue to the soft nipple, slid an arm across her warm body and inhaled the saltiness of her skin. Grace stirred slightly. With a curious sadness, Dawn tightened her embrace.

For the first time in her life she found herself wondering who she really was. It was not something she'd ever thought about. She took for granted her identity — a champion swimmer, a nice girl from a respectable family. Her parents were decent traditional kinds of people. They'd worked hard to send her to the right schools, to pay for the best swimming coach in Sydney. Her father was a good provider, her mother was always there, mostly in the kitchen. They were terribly proud of her. *What a daughter,* her father often said, *what a blessing from the Lord.*

Her parents were religious — not fanatical or anything, just plodding Protestant churchgoers. They blessed meals, read the Bible on Sundays, and told Dawn to keep herself pure for her future husband. She'd ignored them, of course, and Dawn figured they'd eventually resigned themselves to thanking the Lord she'd never got herself pregnant.

Easing out of Grace's arms, she rolled onto her side and stared at the wall. What would they think of this? Of her with a woman? Sex with men was tolerated because eventually it would lead to a husband and children. But with a woman? She would never be able to tell them. Well, she might not have to. She'd done it once . . . twice. So what? That didn't mean she would want to do it with every woman she saw.

But the idea chased her relentlessly. She would do it again, she admitted deep in her heart. What did that mean? The question fluttered and danced in her consciousness until she drifted back into sleep, finally surrendering to the answer. *I'm a lesbian.*

CHAPTER TWELVE

A veil of wan light covered the sky and the watery moon retreated as day broke on the island. Alone on Dawn's veranda, Grace sipped her tea and thought about the woman asleep inside.

One Louis Vuitton trunk coming up, she congratulated herself. The prospect felt oddly flat; in fact it made her downright uneasy. Her skin still tingled with the memory of Dawn. She'd felt so good, so new and fresh. Grace wanted to pleasure her, indulge her, open her and get inside. There was something very alluring about Dawn, about her tentative caresses, her naive astonishment at her own physicality.

Subdued, Grace leaned against the balustrade and rubbed the nape of her neck in an attempt to ease the tension building there. She had to go soon. Cody would be picking her up in her motorboat. Annabel would fly her to Rarotonga. With a sinking feeling, she scanned her lush surroundings. She hadn't realized how quickly she'd come to take the island for granted. Suddenly the enormity of Argus's plan struck her like a physical blow. Until now it had seemed distant and unreal. A set of statistics and calculations. Another handsomely paid deliverable.

Grace cupped her forehead in her hands. How could she calmly recommend the blasting of a coral reef that was home to thousands of creatures, the desecration of the entire island? How could she participate in the wanton destruction of something so precious and beautiful? Because it was her job . . . because someone paid her?

Grace felt sick. Annabel was right. She'd lost all perspective. She probably should have sought professional help years ago.

Annabel had been shocked and horrified at her clinical account of the whole experience. Yet Grace had been absolutely truthful when she said she felt nothing, no emotion at all.

Four years ago she had been raped by four men, left for dead, and had been comatose for six weeks. The police had pieced together the story from the evidence unwittingly provided by her body. Grace still couldn't remember a thing . . . no faces, no voices, nothing. All she had was her Dream and she couldn't even remember that.

Annabel had urged her to see someone when she got back home but Grace wasn't convinced there was much point. Four years had gone by. She enjoyed life. Why take a trip into the past to relive an experience that could only damage her peace of mind? It was not as if she were sexually dysfunctional, after all.

She thought about Dawn, about holding her in the night, seeking comfort from her when she woke sweating from the Dream. Shrugging off a brief sharp sense of loss, she reminded herself that Dawn was just a kid. She was looking for romance, passionate declarations on moonlit beaches. She would pine after Grace for a few days then find some other sweet young thing to hold hands with. Puppy love. It was hardly Grace's style.

Dawn's head was swimming. For a moment she lay very still, then she stared at the pillow next to hers, noting the impression of another head. Her gaze traveled slowly around the room, halting at the window.

Grace was sitting on the veranda, staring out to sea.

Dawn studied her for a long time, then swung her legs to the floor. There was a fluttering in her womb. It was time to say goodbye. It seemed impossible, unreal. They had only just met. Surely what had happened between them was too important, too wonderful to mean nothing.

Belting a silk kimono around her waist, Dawn headed unsteadily out of her room. She felt dizzy. Her hands were clammy and a film of perspiration was collecting across her forehead. A dull insistent pain gathering in her thighs reminded her that she hadn't taken any medication in two days.

In the kitchen, she propped herself against the counter and plunged her hand into the cookie jar. Plain dry biscuits — anything to lift her blood sugar. Then she'd have to dose up. Doggedly she chewed several tasteless crackers in quick succession. They felt hideously insecure in her stomach. She was going to be sick, Dawn realized.

She made it to the bathroom only seconds before she threw up. Footsteps rapidly followed.

"Are you all right, Dawn?" Grace demanded.

"What does it look like?" Facing the woman hovering in the doorway, Dawn immediately wished she could exchange the words for some sweeter, more winning response.

Grace seemed at a loss. "God, you look ill."

It was obvious what she was thinking. *What was wrong with Dawn? Did she have some rare tropical disease? Was it fatal? Was it contagious?* "It's just the DTs," Dawn explained dryly. "I haven't doped up in forty-eight hours."

"Are you saying you're addicted?"

Dawn raised her chin. "I'm saying I'm in pain and I'm weaning myself off my medication."

"Are you sure you should be doing that?" Grace scrutinized her. "I mean, there's no crime in getting relief."

"Sure." Dawn shrugged. "Only I don't want to spend the rest of my life popping pills, that's all."

Grace looked awkward, her eyes straying to Dawn's legs. "Will you ever . . ."

"Walk perfectly again?" Dawn finished on a brittle note. "Probably not. Why do you ask?"

"I just wondered."

Feeble, Grace thought. She had to go, she reminded herself emphatically. This was not the time to begin a deep and meaningful conversation.

They'd moved to the veranda, and now Dawn was staring at her. She looked painfully vulnerable, chin tilted defensively, eyes strangely hopeful. Grace's mouth went dry. Complications.

"Does it matter to you?" Dawn asked.

"Of course it matters," Grace responded carefully. "I like you, Dawn. I want to see you fully recovered."

"Do you?" The response was strained. "Want to see me, I mean?"

Grace sagged back into her chair. "Sure I do." She injected her voice with a lightness she didn't feel. "If you're ever in New York, look me up . . ."

"That's not what I meant," Dawn said.

Grace wished she would stop right there.

"I'm asking if I matter to you." The blue eyes shone bright with emotion. "I'm asking if it meant anything . . . last night . . . ?"

Grace cursed inwardly. She was furious at Dawn all of a sudden. Knowing that Dawn cared for her was too much of a burden. She wanted to say goodbye to Dawn and remember her as two hot nights on a tropical island. That's all.

"I had fun last night," she told Dawn flippantly. "Maybe we can repeat it sometime."

"That's it?" Dawn's face paled.

Grace stood. "Look, I have to go. I'm sorry . . ."

"You feel nothing? Felt nothing?" Dawn's voice radiated disbelief, anger.

Resentful of the defensiveness she felt rising, Grace shoved her feet into her sandals. "I said I enjoyed it, Dawn." She raised her voice slightly. "Can't we just leave it at that, for God's sake. I don't want to hurt you."

"Then why are you lying to me?"

"I'm not lying!" Her voice reverberated across the still morning air.

Dawn's eyes blazed, dark shimmering blue. "I felt something. I felt it here." She slapped her chest with an angry fist. "And so did you. You're just too chicken to admit it!"

"What!" Grace's hands were shaking. This was too much. Why the hell had she waited around here to play Ms. Nice Girl? She should have gone home while the kid was still sleeping. Pinned a goodbye note to the door. "You don't know what you're talking about," she informed Dawn coldly. "I'm the first woman you've ever slept with. That hardly makes you an authority."

"I know what I felt!"

"And I'll tell you what I felt," she retorted. "It's called hot, turned on. I felt lust, Dawn. I wanted to fuck you. End of story."

"I know that. I'm not stupid." Dawn advanced unsteadily toward her and seized a handful of her shirt. Then she was crying. "Grace, please." It came out all broken. "Remember last night, after your dream . . ."

"No!" Grace tore herself free of Dawn's grip, then

watched with horror as the younger woman was thrown off balance.

Dawn staggered back and even as Grace's arm shot out to prevent her, she crashed onto the timber planks with a cry of agony.

"Oh, God . . . Dawn." Grace was on her knees, reaching for her. "Oh, baby. I'm sorry." She cradled the crumpled form, listening helplessly to the small animal grunts of pain.

Then scalding blue eyes met hers and Dawn gasped, "Get my fucking pills, Grace. Then get the hell out of here. I never want to see you again."

Seated on Grace Ramsay's veranda, Cody was so engrossed in her paperback that she didn't notice the copper-haired woman approaching.

"Good book?"

Starting, Cody stared up, shielding her eyes against the sun. Grace was standing in front of her, one hand twitching at her earring, the other hiding in her pocket. Her face looked pale and strained. Attributing this to the shameful circumstances of her departure, Cody felt a brief private pleasure. Served her right.

Cody couldn't pretend to like Grace Ramsay. It was nothing to do with the fact that she was one of Annabel's castoffs. It was Grace's personality. She was so detached, so self-satisfied. And she had the morals of a TV evangelist. Cody made a show of looking at her watch. "You're late," she said bluntly. "Are you ready to leave?"

"Sure. I've just been saying my farewells." Grace idly took the book from Cody's knee and with calm deliberation flipped through a few pages. Meeting Cody's eyes, she observed, "Tama Janowitz ... And I thought urban angst was passé."

Cody snatched the book back. Infuriated at the frank way Grace was looking her up and down, she asked pointedly, "Do you need help with your luggage?"

"I think I can handle it," Grace murmured. She emerged some minutes later, showered and changed. She was holding something out to Cody, her expression that of a cat remembering a puddle of cream. "Annabel left these behind the other night."

Forcing nonchalance, Cody took the sunglasses and jammed them into her pocket. Annabel had every right to spend time with Grace — to find out about this Argus stuff, she reasoned. She trusted her, didn't she? Dragging herself out of her chair, she lifted a couple of the bags and stalked off along the jungle track toward the beach. Grace would soon be gone, she reminded herself. All Cody needed to do was resist the temptation of tipping her overboard.

As she pushed the dinghy into the water, she saw Grace turn and stare back at the beach. Up near the palms there was a flash of pink. Cody waved an oar. "Dawn!" she called, then caught an odd glimmer in Grace's eyes.

The woman looked like she'd just murdered someone's puppy. In the grip of growing suspicion, Cody reviewed the events of the morning.

When she'd gone to Grace's cottage, she'd called out and glanced in the windows that faced onto the veranda. Grace's bed was empty and neatly made.

When Grace had returned she'd taken a shower and changed her clothes, surely the kind of thing you did *before* you went to calling on your neighbor. That is, unless you'd spent the night somewhere else.

Cody eyed Grace. "Have you been sleeping with Dawn?" she demanded accusingly.

Grace's eyes widened. "What's this? Confession?"

"I should have guessed." Cody groaned out loud. "I suppose you just couldn't resist trying your luck."

"And what if I did? What's it to you?"

"Dawn's straight," Cody said sharply.

"Wise up, sweetheart!" Grace gave a brittle laugh. "She might be homophobic but she's definitely not straight."

Grace was speaking firsthand. Appalled, Cody thought about Dawn, unhappy and confused, asking questions about lesbians. "You took advantage of her!" she said angrily.

"Well, someone had to."

The woman was completely degenerate. And she sure as hell rated herself high. "Oh, I see," Cody said. "You did her a favor."

Grace gave a small expressive whistle. "If I didn't know better, I'd think you were jealous. Come to think of it, Annabel mentioned Dawn has the hots for *you.*" She raised an eyebrow. "Why don't you check her out? I've done all the hard work for you, after all."

Cody blinked in disbelief. She couldn't be hearing this. "Grace," she said. "The next time you open your mouth to make a comment like that, you'll be swallowing ocean."

Grace only grinned. "I can see why you made such a big impression on Annabel."

Cody gave her a stony look. "I can see why you didn't."

Chin cradled despondently in her hands, Dawn blew sand off the pages of her Jackie Collins. Over an hour ago she'd watched Cody and Grace skim away across the glistening water. She hadn't cried, and she wasn't going to. Grace Ramsay didn't warrant it.

Face it, Dawn, she told herself unkindly, *you asked for it. You could have saved your pride and said goodbye as if it didn't matter. You could have made no emotional demands.* But she'd taken a risk, hoping the Grace she'd discovered during the night might have lingered. Now she was beginning to think she had imagined her.

Closing her book, she stared broodingly at the empty horizon. She felt drained, years older. So much had happened in so little time. How could she have been so blind? She must have been living in some kind of bubble, thinking the only future she had apart from swimming was marriage and children.

Dawn recalled her last Moon Island holiday and cringed. She had been so obnoxious . . . to Cody in particular. Heat seeped into her cheeks. Even then she'd had a crush on Cody, she recognized miserably. She must have made a complete fool of herself.

A thrumming whine made Dawn look up. A small silver plane was climbing away from the island. Annabel and Grace. Her heart turned over. Were they really having an affair? In the end she had been too chicken to ask. And too busy getting Grace into bed, she reminded herself with abject shame.

Straining to catch the final fading note of the engine, she was conscious of feeling desperately alone. Grace's cottage was empty and she would never see her again. Leaning heavily on her stick, she started along the track to Frangipani Cottage. Maybe she should just go back home to Sydney. There really wasn't any reason to stay. She'd gone quite far enough for one journey of self-discovery, surely.

She reached the cottage, wandered inside, capsized onto her bed, then lurched straight up again, tears of dismay flooding her eyes. She could smell cloves. With a wrenching sob, she abandoned the bed, tearing the sheets from the mattress and throwing them out the door. Then she stared around. The very walls seemed to have trapped the echo of Grace's voice, her sighs, her sensual laughter. Dawn's skin prickled with the memory of her touch, her mouth trembled as if tasting Grace with shocking clarity.

She stared at herself in the mirror and recoiled from the sight of her ripeness. Her body was rounder, her skin pinkly glowing. Knowing eyes confronted her, a full expectant mouth. She was aching and moist, wanting to make love again.

Dawn stumbled out of the room. She couldn't stay here, she thought distractedly. It was unbearable. With clumsy hands she rummaged in the laundry for clean clothes, pulling on loose cotton shorts and a T-shirt. Then she grabbed her small backpack, stuffed a sweater and her water flask into it, and fastened her Reeboks.

Villa Luna was about three and a half hours' walk. Dawn was certain she could remember the way from riding it the other day with Cody. She checked her pack for the compass and pocket knife, went to the bathroom cupboard and removed her painkillers and the little first aid kit.

She wasn't planning on an accident, but it couldn't do any harm to take precautions.

Just before she left, she cranked the ancient telephone for Villa Luna and waited, experimentally flexing her legs. There was no pain. A double dose that morning had taken care of that. No one answered the phone and she deliberated for a second whether to wait and try again, then she dropped it into the cradle.

Cody wouldn't mind if she just turned up. Dawn felt sure of that.

"You can really fly this thing," Grace commented as they taxied to a halt in Avarua.

Annabel didn't bother to respond. The startled tone people used when they commented on her flying always niggled her. She expected such blatant sexism from men, but it was disappointing that a woman of Grace's intelligence didn't know better.

"I'm sorry I can't hang around," she said, helping Grace with her luggage into the airport lounge. "I have some errands to do."

"So, it's goodbye then," Grace said.

Annabel hesitated. "You will think about what I suggested, won't you?"

"I am thinking about it," Grace said quietly. She met Annabel's eyes. "Look, I . . ."

"It's okay," Annabel said. "Really."

The two women stared at each other, then Grace said, "Will you do me a favor?" She scrawled something on a piece of paper and folded it across the middle. "Will you give this to Dawn?"

Annabel tucked the note thoughtfully into her jacket. "You haven't been messing about with youthful emotions have you, Grace?"

"She's very cute," Grace responded with a shadowed version of her lopsided grin.

Envisaging the scenario, Annabel grimaced. "Pick on someone your own size next time."

"If I'd known she was so —" Grace halted on a defensive note.

"So what?"

Grace looked uncomfortable. "Never mind. Maybe I've got a hang-up or something."

"Remarkable observation."

"I didn't want to hurt her."

Annabel compressed her lips. "Grace," she said mildly. "They're going to put that on your tombstone." She bent forward, kissed her one-time lover lightly on the mouth and murmured goodbye.

"Don't forget the note," Grace called after her.

Three hours later Annabel stuck her head into the hangar. "Smithy?"

The place was dead quiet, no sign of Bevan's elderly mechanic. Puzzled, Annabel strolled across to the Dominie. The plane had obviously been serviced. Smithy had turned it around ready for take-off, and the cargo was fully loaded. He usually waited until she was airborne before he packed up for the day.

Just as Annabel was clambering aboard, she spotted a wiry figure waving at her as he advanced across the tarmac. "Lucky I caught yer, ma'am." Smithy thrust a small parcel at her. " 'Mergency drop," he explained with his customary economy of communication. "Mitiaro."

Annabel examined the parcel with a sinking heart. It bore a Red Cross seal and was flagged urgent. "This is going to take hours," she groaned.

The mechanic eyed her sympathetically. "Just missed the tourist charter," he rasped. "Some darn fool forgot to give it to 'em."

Annabel dropped the parcel onto the seat. She couldn't refuse to take it. Bevan operated an informal emergency shuttle around the islands, dropping medical supplies and performing the occasional porcine cesarean. She supposed she should be grateful she'd been spared the latter.

"Well, I'd better give her some stick," she grumbled, belting herself in. The trip would take four hours out of her schedule and if anything went wrong refueling on Mitiaro, she'd be stuck there overnight.

Smithy ran his gnarled fingers across the Dominie's undercarriage then reached inside his overalls. "I've logged yer flight plan." He handed Annabel a dog-eared copy. "The old trooper's runnin' like a dream."

Annabel clipped the plan to her board. "You

know," she sighed. "There are times when I think a Lear wouldn't be such a bad idea after all."

Smithy examined her as if she'd just taken leave of her senses. "For them as can't fly a real plane, maybe," he snorted.

CHAPTER THIRTEEN

Dawn stared up at the sun and hoisted her T-shirt out of her shorts, using the hem to mop the sweat beaded over her face. She'd been walking for two hours and, having crossed the northeastern ridge, was now picking her way through the dense jungle in the center of the island.

Checking her compass and her watch, she smiled at her own progress. Who said Dawn Beaumont was a write-off? She remembered the last time she had crossed the *makatea*. She had been with two other women and they were returning to Villa Luna after sheltering from the hurricane. One of the women was injured and they'd had to carry her part of the way.

They'd gotten hopelessly lost after some fool dropped the compass, and Dawn had wondered if they would ever make it. Back then it had seemed impossible. Now, Dawn was amazed she could have been so frightened. Moon Island was a tiny little place. You could walk from one side to the other in a day. Even if you did get lost, you only had to head for the ocean and take the long route around the island.

The only real danger was the *makatea,* the fossilized coral reef that circled the center of the island. Although it was overgrown with jungle, the ancient coral was still razor sharp. But so long as you watched your step you couldn't really go wrong.

By Dawn's calculations, Villa Luna was about an hour and a half away. Guessing she must be somewhere near the cave they had sheltered in during the hurricane, she examined her surroundings with a surge of excitement. The jungle had a frightening uniformity about it. Thank God for compasses and pocketknives, Dawn reflected, carving a notch into the palm she'd been leaning against. Glancing again at her watch, she thought about finding the Kopeka Cave. There was plenty of time and the idea was oddly tempting.

She'd give it half an hour, she decided, and if she hadn't located it, she would simply carry on to Villa Luna.

* * * * *

Bleary-eyed, Cody plucked her paperback off her chest and crossed the sitting room to gaze out the window. Annabel wouldn't be back for hours. She really should go outside instead of lying about like a couch potato. She could go fishing or maybe just hoon around in the boat. The new outboard was really something. Two hundred horsepower. Time to dust off the water skis.

Wondering if Dawn was home, she tried the phone. No answer. Doubtless she was consoling herself with Jackie Collins. She wouldn't mind company. God only knew the poor woman could probably use someone to talk to if she'd just come off second-best with Grace Ramsay. Gathering up her fishing gear and her bathing suit, Cody wrote a note to Annabel and headed for the beach.

The runabout was hot from the afternoon sun. Chugging out of Passion Bay, Cody enjoyed the breeze in her face and hair. Sometimes the heat of the tropics got to her. After Wellington, with its long winters and bitter Southerlies, Moon Island felt like a permanent hothouse. Every now and then she found herself yearning for a cold, miserable day just for old time's sake.

She anchored off Hibiscus Bay, changed into her sedate swimsuit and swam ashore. The beach was empty, no sign of Dawn. Calling her name, Cody strolled into the jungle toward Frangipani Cottage.

The place looked deserted. Cody knocked on the front door, walked around the cottage, then flopped down on a chair, a crawling uneasiness overtaking her. She stared at the silent cottage, full of misgivings. What if it had all been too much for

Dawn ... the accident, her ruined career, seduction by the sleazy Grace? Could she have done Something Stupid?

Latching firmly onto the negative fantasy, Cody's imagination generated a bloody suicide in a bath, a comatose Dawn clutching an empty sleeping-pill bottle. She lurched to her feet, pushed open the unlocked door and barged indoors, shouting Dawn's name. Her frantic eyes took in an empty sitting room, the Jackie Collins face down on the coffee table. She stumbled over a pile of sheets in front of the bedroom door and stared around the room. Nothing, just a faint whiff of spicy perfume.

Frowning, Cody scoured the cottage. She pulled open the bathroom cabinet, slammed the mirrored door, then paused and opened it again. Where was the first aid kit? And Dawn's pills. She definitely kept them on that shelf. Returning to the bedroom, she tripped over Dawn's sandals and caught a sharp image of the younger woman tying her Reeboks the day she came out fishing. Where were they? She rummaged in the bedroom closet, gazed around the veranda, then, in puzzled silence, considered the clues.

Dawn wasn't at home, she was wearing her Reeboks, she had taken the first aid kit and her painkillers. A hot-shot detective like Amanda Valentine might have drawn some dazzling conclusion from all of that, but Cody merely felt baffled. She would wait, she decided, retreating onto the veranda steps and contemplating the ocean. And if Dawn wasn't back in a couple of hours, she would just have to go and look for her.

* * * * *

Simmering with frustration, Grace checked into the Rarotongan Resort Hotel. It was just her luck — stuck for three days before she could get a plane out! All this and the deal was off anyway. By now Hausmann would have ceased licking his wounds and would doubtless be cultivating some military dictator looking to trade land for firepower. Grace couldn't see why Argus didn't simply expand its Mexican dumping operation. But Hausmann was hellbent on a Pacific presence. It would make Argus so very attractive to the Japanese — clients and investors alike.

Grace wondered gloomily how many more islands she would have to assess, how many more reports she would write. Somehow she was finding the entire business increasingly unappetizing. Where would it end? What kind of world would it be when there were no more islands to destroy and no more rainforests to convert to cheap packaging?

Feeling jaded, she phoned New York.

Camille Marquez took the call. Hausmann, she explained, was in Tokyo finalizing the first big dumping contract for Moon Island.

"What?" Grace was taken aback. "I understood the deal went cold."

There was a pause. "I think you should talk with Mr. Hausmann about this."

"Are you saying the owner has agreed to sell?" Grace demanded.

"I'm saying as far as I know the project is proceeding as planned," Camille replied coolly.

"Well." Grace forced neutrality into her tone.

"Evidently you have information I don't." After supplying Camille with her arrival details, Grace hung up.

In the few hours since they arrived in Rarotonga, Annabel couldn't possibly have changed her mind. And if she had ... Grace warded off images of the island leveled, danger signs everywhere, the reef filled with suppurating waste. Anxiously twisting her earring, she called a taxi and strode from her room.

Annabel had flown to Mitiaro a few times on mercy dashes with Bevan. The island was the smallest of the volcanic group lying northeast of Rarotonga. Tourists didn't bother with it much. It was flat and mostly swamp, and there was nothing to eat except eels and bananas. A couple of hundred islanders subsisted there and every now and then someone had an accident and the local dispensary called Rarotonga for supplies. It was a good excuse to gossip on the wireless, and to entice a pilot to airlift additional goodies from Avarua.

After a couple of hours, Annabel started watching for the familiar dotting of islands that signaled her destination. Theoretically she should be right over Atiu, with Bevan's and Don's place a mere pineapple's toss away. She peered out at the turquoise ocean, removed her aviators, squinted around, then put them back on and studied her instruments.

She was bearing northeast at two thousand feet, dead on course. Yet there was no island in sight. She tapped her compass lightly. The reading was unchanged. Shrugging she radioed Mitiaro. A cloud of static hissed back at her. She checked her frequency and the radio whined in protest. Niggled, she examined her flight plan.

Everything seemed straightforward. She was on course, on time and supposedly just minutes away from landing on Mitiaro's dilapidated little strip. She glanced at her fuel gauge, then stared, riveted. Full. It read full. Impossible. She tapped the dial sharply. The needle appeared to be stuck.

"Oh hell," she cursed.

Dropping a few hundred feet, she made a conscious effort to control her leaping pulse and collect her wits. The horizon spread before her, barren shimmering blue, and suddenly Annabel thought that an empty ocean must be the loneliest place on earth to fly a plane over. Amelia Earhart had done it, and Jean Batten and hundreds of other aviators, some of them in craft that made the Dominie look as advanced as a Stealth Bomber.

Mitiaro was one of a group of islands. Assuming she was no more than a few degrees off course one way or the other, she should still be able to sight them. Annabel gazed ahead, willing an island to rise from the sleeping ocean.

There was probably some simple explanation, she reasoned, a silly error on the flight plan. If she could just locate it and work her way backward, calculate her position ... She still had fuel, even if her gauge had malfunctioned. The Dominie's range was nearly five hundred miles. It was just enough to get her back to Rarotonga ... if she turned back straightaway, that was. And if her bearings were correct.

Frowning, she banked right, half circled, banked left. There was nothing, just ocean. She looked hard at her compass and suddenly she felt sick. If her compass was to be believed, the sun was in the wrong place. Instrument failure? Annabel rapidly performed some mental gymnastics. She had around a hundred minutes of fuel left. If she climbed a little and worked with the slight tailwind she could drop her airspeed back to around ninety and maybe stretch her air time to two hours max. Surely she could locate at least one of the Cook Islands in that time. Tuning into the International Distress Frequency, she put out a CQ. There was no reply. She tried again, only this time registered an SOS, then she just flew.

As time crept by she found herself listening with painful concentration for the telltale splutter of an engine dying. You're going to die, she thought numbly, then rejected the idea. It couldn't happen. It was too unfair. Cody's face materialized before her, gray eyes appealing. *Do you have to fly so much. I worry about you terribly.*

Annabel was stricken. What if this really was the end? What if she never saw Cody again, never held her. There would be no goodbye, no chance to tell her how much she loved her. A dry sob wrenched at her throat and she found herself bargaining with God. *Please don't let me die, I'll do anything . . .*

Wet with sweat, she studied her watch. She had fifteen minutes of fuel left. If she was lucky. The barren ocean taunted her anew and she logged yet another mayday, desperately conscious of being unable to state her position. Her omni was depressingly silent, not entirely surprising given the nearest VOR station was probably out of range. She wondered if anyone had picked up her signal, if, by some miracle, she could ditch her plane into the ocean and survive. Would she even be found?

She groped beneath her seat, found a dusty life jacket and slipped it over her head. Then she began to replay with icy detachment everything Bevan Mitchell had ever taught her about crash landings. On water . . . glide in, belly flop, get out immediately or head up the tail and hack your way out. All of the Dominie's weight was up front. She would hit the water, float for a few seconds, then nosedive.

Annabel felt about inside her clothing, located her Swiss Army knife and congratulated herself on being prepared for anything. She could open a can, kill a fish, reflect the sun off an open blade to attract the attention of a rescue craft. In short, survival was child's play. She laughed, a harsh hollow sound. Her eyes fixed dully on the horizon, she imagined herself in Cody's arms, felt her warmth so vividly that a curious calm settled on her. She thought of Boston, her parents, Aunt Annie. She thought about her lonely childhood, her crazy working life, then Moon Island and Cody. Oh my love, she thought bitterly. How could fate be so cruel?

There was a spluttering cough and she gazed wildly at her right wing. She was running out of petrol. In a few minutes the Dominie would start losing altitude, it would glide for a while, unlike a modern aircraft, then it would drop lower and lower until it plunged into the ocean.

Annabel straightened her back. They said drowning was a painless way to go. She stared dubiously at the ocean and blinked with disbelief.

Directly ahead of her a gray-green blemish intruded on the endless blue. A mirage? She dropped height, tried to ignore the hiccup of a propeller, reached for her binoculars.

A tiny atoll lay some six or seven tantalizing minutes ahead of her. Annabel could make out the pink circle of a reef, a milky blue lagoon, white sand, clusters of palm trees. She could almost hear Bevan. *Have you ever flown a glider, kid? That's what you've got when you've got no power.*

Dropping height, she eased back the throttle, tossing up the idea of ditching the Dominie in the lagoon or plowing into the beach. On the face of it, the lagoon seemed the obvious choice, but Annabel had never been much of a swimmer and somehow dry land seemed more of a known quantity. Annabel assessed the thin white belt of sand. Landing on a soft surface, a somersault was the worst hazard. You had to land nose up, but not so far up that you smashed your tail. Or you had to risk a deliberate belly flop, smashing your undercarriage so the plane would just grind to a halt.

Banking left a few degrees, she straightened and almost laughed as her engines spluttered and died. Minutes later the Dominie swanned into the white sand, absorbing the impact with a sickening crunch. Undercarriage crumpling like paper, the little silver plane plowed violently along the beach, one wing skimming the tide, the other closing fast on a stand of palms.

The clearance just wasn't there. Collecting a tree trunk with one wing, it spun about face, and with a hideous tearing sound, the fuselage ripped apart. When finally the Dominie came to rest, its tail had separated completely, its nose was buried in sand, and inside the cockpit Annabel smiled once, then slumped over the column, a pool of blood gathering around her feet.

CHAPTER FOURTEEN

Grace stumbled through the hangar doorway and yelled, "Hello! Is anybody there?"

From the opposite wall a small, grizzled-looking man in a white overall peered over his shoulder. "Lookin' fer someone, miss?"

"You're from London!" Grace exclaimed, moving inside.

"John Smith at yer service," he rasped. "You obviously 'aven't been living at 'ome fer a fair while."

"No, I live in New York. I'm Grace Ramsay."

The old man eyed her sharply. "Wotcha doin' livin' in that 'ellhole 'cross the Atlantic, then?"

Grace grinned. "Leading a life of moral decay, Mr. Smith."

"They call me Smithy roun' these parts." A pair of bright sparrow-eyes sized her up. "You lookin' for 'erself?"

"Annabel Worth? Yes. I need to see her urgently."

"Too late." He shook his head. "Flew out a few hours back. But the guvnor's due any time. Need a ride, I daresay 'e'll oblige."

The governor? Annabel had mentioned a pilot she employed. "No. I don't need a ride," she said. "I'm staying here on Rarotonga."

"Yer weren't out 'ere lookin' for 'er before?"

Grace shook her head. Before?

"Jes' wonderin'. Found these." He reached into a pocket and produced a pair of pliers.

Grace turned them over in her hand. "Not mine."

Smithy pocketed them indifferently. "Finders keepers."

Losers weepers. Grace thought again about Robert Hausmann. Surely Annabel hadn't changed her mind about selling. "Smithy," she said. "Can we contact Annabel on Moon Island?"

He scratched his head. "Won't be there yet. She'll be on Mitiaro, I reckon."

"Mitiaro?"

"Northern Group ... 'mergency medical drop. We could radio."

Grace brightened. Annabel would probably laugh at her. Perhaps Camille had it all wrong. And besides, what was she going to do if Annabel had decided to sell? Make some groveling plea for conservation?

Increasingly daunted, she listened as Smithy radioed the island and conducted a conversation in some strange code. There was a curious shift in his expression and as he signed off, his eyes met Grace's and something in them made her mouth dry.

"What is it . . ." she began.

Smithy's weathered face was grim. "Not there," he said stiffly. " 'Asn't arrived."

Dawn eased herself into the mouth of the Kopeka Cave, blinking rapidly to accustom herself to the dimness. The cave was not completely dark. Daylight shafted into the limestone chambers through a series of narrow chimneys which also provided conduits for the thousands of Kopeka birds that made their home in the cave. There was a flurry of wings as Dawn padded into the fusty interior and the tiny swallows swooped low, strafing her like bats. Waving her arms, she shooed them off. Somehow they didn't bother her as much as they had the last time.

When she reached the hollow where they had sat the night of the hurricane, she nudged the ancient remains of a fire with her toe. Was it the one she had built after Cody left them? What a pig she'd been back then, Dawn thought, remembering her loud complaints and inconsiderate remarks to her companions. Sitting opposite the long dead embers, she stared up at the limestone ceiling. She never noticed how pretty it was, how the caves amplified sound.

She called out her name again and again until it resonated through the connecting caverns. Then she giggled at the childish impulse and took a long drink from her water flask. She was hungry, she realized suddenly, starving in fact. She'd felt so sick when she fled the cottage that it hadn't occurred to her to bring any food. Mouth watering, Dawn recalled the bananas she'd seen drooping from the palms around the cave. They couldn't be that hard to reach.

She scrambled to her feet and returned to the brilliance of the afternoon. There was a palm only a few yards away. Dawn's attention fastened greedily on an enormous bunch of stubby pinkish bananas. Clutching awkwardly at the fleshy protrusions that laddered the thick trunk, she grappled her way toward the fruit.

The bananas fell with satisfying thuds into the foliage below. When she had accounted for at least twenty or so, Dawn slithered down to the ground and set about retrieving them. Then she sat down beside her cache and gobbled them happily. The pink bananas were smaller and sweeter than the yellow kind. Lady fingers, they were called. Suddenly Dawn found that concept extremely titillating. Giggling at her train of thought, she gathered up the remaining few bananas and stuffed them into her pack for the walk to Villa Luna.

Only minutes later the first violent pains struck. Panting, she collapsed against a papaya, her mind instantly flooded with garbled ideas about food poisoning and tropical diseases. The pain was excruciating, stabbing her directly below her ribs where twelve poorly chewed bananas had descended on her empty Voltarin-damaged stomach. A classic case of banana belly.

Groaning, Dawn curled herself into a ball and started crying with frustration. Why couldn't anything go right for her? What had she ever done that was so terrible she had to pay for it with wrecking her legs, turning into some kind of sexual weirdo and now dying of banana poisoning in the middle of nowhere?

Her father would say the Lord moves in mysterious ways.

"Bastard!" Dawn yelled.

The late afternoon sun lolled low in the sky. Cody trudged through the jungle, worried and irritated at the same time. She had already wasted a couple of hours pacing Dawn's veranda and scouring the beaches. She'd even tried Grace's cottage. In the end she'd decided to go and look for her.

If Dawn had taken a walk, she might easily have met with an accident or got herself lost. In fact, the more Cody thought about it, the more obvious it seemed. Depressed, Dawn had plunged off into the jungle, and all too soon she'd lost her way. By now she could be anywhere on the island. Cody tried not to picture her bleeding to death at the bottom of some gully, having fallen on the *makatea*.

It came as quite a surprise when she found the first piece of white rag tied to a papaya leaf. A few paces farther, there was a notch in a tree trunk, then another bit of rag. Despite herself, Cody was impressed. The Dawn of three years ago would never have considered such practicalities; certainly no one planning on a quiet suicide somewhere in the jungle would bother leaving a trail.

With new confidence, she followed the freshly trampled vegetation. Her quarry appeared to be heading toward the center of the island. It all made sense now. Needing a shoulder to cry on, Dawn had decided to walk to Villa Luna. Maybe she was already there.

Cody stopped in her tracks. It would be foolish to keep on walking if Dawn was twiddling her thumbs at Villa Luna. Besides, Annabel was due back soon. Fanning herself with a papaya leaf, Cody headed back toward the beach. Grace Ramsay, she thought grimly. This entire fiasco was her fault.

In the runabout it took twenty minutes to reach Villa Luna. Dawn wasn't there and neither was Annabel. Pacing the veranda, Cody glumly examined the sky. She tried not to worry. It wouldn't be the first time Annabel had got stuck on Raro, waiting for some repair job. Bits were always falling off that damned Dominie.

At least Bevan would be back soon, she consoled herself. They'd had a message that he'd bought another plane. She could picture it already: grunty motors, a flashy high-tech instrument panel and comfortable seats. At last they could put that old hack out to pasture. Then at least if Annabel had to fly something, it would be modern and well-equipped. The prospect failed to enthrall her, and for about the thousandth time Cody wished Annabel would hang up her aviators and get herself a safe hobby. What was wrong with knitting?

Reclining on the veranda steps, she inhaled the twilight smell of the jungle. Annabel wouldn't be coming now. She never flew this late. But what about Dawn? There was barely enough light to saddle up Kahlo and look for her. Cody sighed loudly. Why couldn't other people be like her? She didn't have dangerous hobbies, she didn't limp off with a walking stick on some jungle trek. Sometimes she felt like the only normal person in town.

Stuffing a pillow behind her head, she took her paperback off the table and contemplated its jacket for a moment. Urban angst! That fake bitch Grace Ramsay should talk.

As dusk closed on Avarua, Grace followed Smithy back to the hangar. "I just can't believe this!" she exploded. "A freighter reports an SOS three hundred miles out of here and nobody does a thing. What sort of outfit is this?"

They had no flight plans filed for that area, the Air Traffic Controller had said ineffectually. Ms. Worth was bound for Mitiaro, nowhere near the location of the distress signal. He'd shown them a map of bare sea and drawn a ring around the area. No, they weren't planning a search at this stage.

He'd notified Silk and Boyd, of course. They had a freighter going out there in a few days and they'd promised to take a look.

"But she was supposed to have landed on Mitiaro hours ago!" Grace cried. "What are they waiting for!"

Smithy wiped a gnarled hand across his thin gray hair. "Thing I can't fathom, is why them bleedin' plans were filed."

"What do you mean?

"They was stamped," the mechanic rasped. "Arrival confirmed."

"You mean . . ." Grace could hardly believe what she was hearing. "Someone marked that she had arrived when she hadn't?"

Smithy nodded.

"So when the SOS came in there was no way they could make the connection. Oh, my God," she whispered. "She's crashed." Stuffing her hands into her pockets, she paced the hangar. "We can't just stand around here and do nothing!"

The little mechanic seemed smaller than ever. He was crying, Grace realized. "We better radio Moon Island," he finally mumbled. "Could be she changed 'er plans."

Grace froze. What would they say to Cody if Annabel wasn't there? She felt physically sick at the prospect. You couldn't just radio someone and tell her the woman she loved had probably crashed her plane. Her mind wandered to Annabel. Dead? Was it possible?

Shaken, she faced Smithy. "I can't do it. We need to go out there."

Smithy was preoccupied. "Listen." He raised a silencing hand and walked outside, head cocked.

Grace traipsed after him. She couldn't hear a thing. Just the occasional birdcall, car motors firing, the sound of voices somewhere, a child crying.

"It's the guvnor," Smithy announced after another minute of silence.

Grace surveyed the graying sky without optimism. "I can't see anything."

"Nor'east." Smithy pointed.

Either he had X-ray vision or he was going senile, Grace decided. "I could go and see about chartering a plane," she volunteered.

"Won't be needin' that," she was told.

As she prepared to argue, she saw it too, the faintest speck. Riveted, she focused her attention on the tiny black spot. Then she heard a faint hum. Relief pounded through her limbs.

Smithy extracted a packet of cigarettes from his top pocket and offered her one. Grace took it. They watched the speck draw nearer and nearer, then Grace turned startled eyes on her companion as he suddenly let out a long whistle, stubbed out his cigarette and rushed off into the hangar.

He returned a split second later with a pair of chocks and a huge tobacco-stained grin. " 'E went and done it," he muttered under his breath as they watched the plane descend. "Ain't she a beauty?"

CHAPTER FIFTEEN

Violet Hazel was talking to herself. Although it was a habit to which she had resigned herself, she had never entirely accepted it. At the age of seventy the specter of senility loomed all too large. What could once be put down to eccentricity suddenly assumed more sinister connotations.

"You're Lucy Adams." Violet addressed the pale-haired woman on the bed. She could remember the child so well, a fairylike creature with white hair and the most astonishing lavender eyes.

Violet had been living on Rarotonga, working as a nurse. That was how she had come to meet the two women who lived on Moon Island, Rebecca and Annie. They used to bring the child in for checkups as often as they could catch the steamer. What a pair they were, dark-haired Rebecca dressed exactly like a man and smoking those thin cigars, Annie with her debutante mannerisms and wicked sense of humor.

Stroking her guest's hair, Violet sighed. It had been such a tragedy, Rebecca leaving for Boston, never to return, killed in a car accident. Then later, Annie and the little girl had left. Over the subsequent years, Violet had often wondered what became of them. For a time she had received letters from Annie — strange disjointed ramblings. They were living with a married sister of hers, Violet recalled vaguely. Eventually the letters had stopped. Then Violet had moved to Solarim and she'd been there ever since.

With an air of professional satisfaction, she probed the jagged cut on the girl's skull. After all these years she hadn't forgotten how to suture. She lifted an eyelid and shone her little torch into the pupil. Her patient had been swinging in and out of consciousness throughout the night. Apart from her head injuries, she had survived her plane crash remarkably unscathed. It remained to be seen whether there was permanent brain damage. She could easily hemorrhage and never wake.

That would be dreadful, Violet thought. She was so much looking forward to having someone else to talk to for a change.

161

* * * * *

Frustrated, Cody sank down beside the radio set, willing it to burst into life. It was only eight in the morning, she reasoned. Annabel was probably stuck on Raro with water in her fuel. Cody could imagine her kicking her heels, waiting for Smithy to get the Dominie going again. It wouldn't be the first time.

If only they had normal telephone communications. They kept meaning to organize it but somehow there were always other priorities. Well, such were the joys of life on a bunch of islands in the Pacific. There was no point in worrying, Cody told herself, then started violently as someone yelled her name.

There was a thrashing sound from the foliage opposite the villa and Cody reached the veranda just in time to see a bedraggled figure emerge from the undergrowth. "Dawn! " Her jaw dropped.

The younger woman was a sorry sight, clothes and skin stained bright green, her face and hands filthy, and her hair tangled with leaves and vines.

With a wide grin, she hobbled toward the veranda, heaved herself up the steps and dropped into a chair, demanding, "Well, aren't you going to offer me a drink?"

Flabbergasted, Cody retreated indoors and returned with a large glass of juice, handing it wordlessly to her visitor.

Pausing between gulps, Dawn announced, "I went to the Kopeka Cave. And I got sick from eating too many bananas, so I had to sleep the night in the jungle."

"You were out overnight?" Cody was mortified. She should have looked again for Dawn after all. How could she have been so negligent? Something might have happened to her ... something obviously had.

The young woman was still prattling happily, "I never thought I could do it. I walked all that way with my legs like this ... Isn't it incredible?"

"Yes," Cody affirmed weakly. "Incredible." She thought about the Dawn of three years ago. Even in perfect health she wouldn't have tried to cross the island on foot. "Why did you do it?" she asked.

"I'm not really sure." A little of Dawn's sparkle faded. "I guess I wanted company. I was feeling upset."

"About Grace?"

Dawn blushed beneath the grime. "You know ..." She gave a small self-effacing laugh. "You must think it's just hilarious ... after the way I've behaved all this time."

"No, I don't think that at all, Dawn," Cody said quietly.

"Well, I feel pretty stupid." Bitterness crept into Dawn's voice. "I know I didn't mean anything to Grace, but I guess I wanted ..." The words wouldn't form and slow tears made rivulets in the dirt on her cheeks.

What *did* she want, Dawn wondered bleakly. Her feelings were in such a mess she didn't know. All she knew was that if Grace walked out of the jungle right now wearing that lopsided grin of hers, she would go weak at the knees with longing. She would drool like an idiot, blindly discard her self-respect and snatch whatever crumbs Grace chose to offer. How humiliating.

Cody was watching her with a sympathetic expression and Dawn felt even more abased, knowing how transparent she must seem. Jerking to her feet, she asked, "Can I use your shower?"

Cody followed her inside. "I'll get a change of clothes for you. I think you're about Annabel's size." Her voice caught as she said it, and Dawn looked at her. Casting a glance in the direction of the radio, she explained in a tight voice, "Annabel didn't arrive back from Raro yesterday. I guess she must be stuck there. She's always having fuel problems and stuff."

Dawn tried to control her expression. Grace and Annabel? Surely they wouldn't have run off together. No. Annabel might be playing around but she was far too classy to do a tacky thing like that.

Cody was staring at her. "Dawn . . ."

Avoiding the fear in those eyes, Dawn turned away. "Look, I really need that shower," she said. "Why don't you radio Rarotonga?"

Grace's heart was pumping and her feet beat a steady tattoo on the concrete pathway. She veered onto a track that disappeared into the deep shadows thrown by a stand of firs. When the first man crossed her path, Grace paid no attention, skirting him to take the leafy track upward.

"Hey, what's the hurry?" he called after her, and Grace lengthened her stride a little.

In another few minutes she would reach open space again. She usually avoided this part of the park, but tonight she had a dinner date and the trees were a shortcut.

"Hey, babe. Got a light?" Another man emerged, blocking the narrow track.

"Sorry. Don't smoke." Grace detoured around a tree to avoid him. He blocked her path again, laughing softly. The smell of whiskey and sour tobacco sullied the green air.

Grace glanced sideways. The slope was steep, but she could make it down there through the trees and circle back. The road was close. Turning abruptly, she dodged the man, knees jarring as she made the rapid descent.

"Hey, guys," she heard. "She's all yours."

Someone grabbed at her. Thrown off balance she crashed heavily into a tree, felt a tearing sensation in her ankle, and reached for a low branch. Before she could get her footing, she was on the ground and hot hands encircled her throat. Struggling, she watched three men emerge from the surrounding trees.

"Please," she croaked when the grip on her throat loosened. "Let me go and I won't make any trouble for you. C'mon guys, you've had your fun."

"Oh no, we ain't." Mean dark eyes taunted her. "The fun's just beginnin'. Ain't that right, boys?"

Then Grace screamed. And screamed. And nobody heard her. And then she couldn't scream any more because they tied a strip of her singlet around her mouth.

Much later Grace felt something on her face, and smiled. A big soft golden Labrador lay down beside her. Clouds swirled, dense and shapeless. There were voices. The dog was barking.

"Don't go," Grace begged it wordlessly. "Please don't leave me here alone."

Bells rang. A telephone.

Grace jerked bolt upright. Her sheets were soaked with sweat. She grabbed for the phone, shivering as the damp sheen evaporated from her skin.

It was Bevan, Annabel's pilot. They would be leaving for Moon Island in an hour.

Grace said she would be ready. Drained, she paced into the bathroom and touched her reflection in the mirror. When she could no longer look, she stood beneath the torrid blast of the shower and soaped herself compulsively.

Dawn stood slack-jawed beside Cody as the plane screeched to a halt and taxied along the pitted strip. Painted dark green, with a pinup girl embellishing the fuselage, it looked exactly like something out of an old war movie. As she and Cody drew closer, Dawn made out the words *Lonesome Lady* painted along the side. She stole an apprehensive glance at Cody.

"What is it?" Cody asked as the pilot dropped to the ground in front of them.

Bevan Mitchell tucked his aviators into his top pocket. "She's a Mitchell B-Seventeen — a genuine warbird."

Cody eyeballed him as though he were speaking in tongues. "Where's Annabel?" she demanded.

The pilot's eyes darted to the cockpit and Dawn held her breath. Grace Ramsay had emerged and was approaching. Something in her expression made Dawn feel nauseated.

"We have some bad news." Grace shoved her hands into her pockets and looked at Cody. "Annabel's missing."

"Missing?" The color fled Cody's face. "What do you mean, missing?"

"She left Raro for Mitiaro Island yesterday," Bevan said. "She never arrived. There was a distress signal picked up three hundred miles southwest of Rarotonga about an hour and a half after she left."

"So what does that mean?" Cody croaked. "Where is she?"

Bevan was visibly shaken. "A search is underway. We'll join in, of course . . ."

"I don't understand." Cody's tone rose sharply, and Dawn moved instinctively toward her. She could feel Grace's piercing regard, sense a pleading in the angle of her head, the nervous shift of her feet.

"Cody," Bevan said with obvious difficulty. "It's almost certain she's crashed. And because of the location it's going to be hard to spot the wreckage."

Cody was gazing at him, stupefied.

"What do you mean about the location?" Dawn asked.

"It's just ocean," he said tautly. "There's nowhere to land."

Cody shook her head. "No!" she shouted, her face parchment white, eyes wild with shock. "It can't be true. I don't believe it!"

* * * * *

Twelve hours later Grace knocked on the door of Dawn's hotel room in Rarotonga. She felt hesitant, less than her usual assured self.

"What do you want?" Dawn asked her abruptly.

She took a couple of paces into the room, her eyes seeking Dawn's. "Can we talk?"

Dawn hedged, obviously avoiding the question. "Cody's asleep in her room," she said stiffly. "The doctor gave her a sedative."

Unspoken words hung heavily between them. The search that afternoon had yielded only an empty sea. Tomorrow they would resume at daybreak, across a wider radius. According to Bevan, there was almost no hope of locating her. Even if by some miracle she had survived a crash, she probably couldn't have lasted two days in the water.

Grace lifted a hand to her eyes. For a moment she was sure she felt tears, but her fingers came back dry. "Poor Cody," she said. She felt a sob rise, fall. Then she was numb again.

Dawn was studying her with bright accusing eyes. Finally she burst out, "What do you care?"

"I care." Grace swallowed with difficulty. "Annabel and I were —"

"Yes, I know all about you and Annabel!" Dawn cut her short, lurching to her feet and cracking her walking stick viciously against the bed. "I know you were having an affair behind Cody's back. But if you say anything to her, I'll . . ." She whacked the bed again. "I'll flatten you."

In any other situation Grace would have laughed at the fierce threat. But the bizarre accusation momentarily stunned her. Dawn was glaring at her, chin tilted, and knuckles white.

"Dawn. I don't know what you're talking about," Grace said. "Annabel and I aren't —"

Dawn promptly swung her stick in the air and thwacked it down at Grace's feet.

"Dawn!" Grace leapt out of the way. "Jesus Christ. Stop it!"

"No! You stop it!" Dawn shouted. "Stop lying to me. I saw you that night."

"What are you talking about? What night?"

Dawn flung her stick across the room. "You're disgusting," she said. "I don't know how you can keep on pretending at a time like this. Annabel is probably dead!"

"Dawn!" Grace raked exasperated fingers through her hair. "Will you *please* explain yourself. When did you see me with Annabel?"

"The next night." Dawn's face was tight. "The night after we . . . slept together."

The night Annabel had come around to order her off the island. The night Grace had told her what happened five years ago. "You were there?" Grace asked Dawn flatly. How much had she heard?

The younger woman's eyes blazed. "Yes, I was. Stupid gooey-eyed little me. I wanted to see you and I hung around at home waiting and waiting, then I went to your place." She pushed a balled fist roughly across her eyes. "And when I got there . . ."

"You saw me and Annabel on the veranda and

you decided we were having sex," Grace concluded on a hard note.

"Well, weren't you?"

"Oh, Dawn." Obviously she hadn't overheard the conversation. She'd just seen them and drawn her own conclusions. Grace ran a weary hand across her forehead. She hardly knew where to begin. "Annabel and I are not lovers," she said. "We were once, six years ago. Now we're just friends." And barely that, thanks to her job. "I was upset about something that night. Annabel was comforting me." Why was she explaining all this? Suddenly Grace felt infuriated with herself. Who cared what some silly kid wanted to believe?

"You were upset," Dawn taunted. "Why? Did she turn you down?"

Grace ordered herself to remain calm and virtuous, a credit to her Karate Sempei, to exercise self-control in the face of severe provocation, to demonstrate the spirit of perseverance . . . "What if she did?" she shouted. "It's none of your goddamned business, anyway!"

"Oh, I'm sorry," Dawn responded sarcastically. "I forgot for a minute. I forgot I'm not supposed to feel anything. I forgot that the name of the game is meaningless sex."

"You didn't have any complaints."

"I didn't have any sense!" Dawn bit the words off abruptly and followed with a forced half-laugh, which only served to reveal her further.

An embarrassed silence followed. Grace's mouth felt dry. She wanted to offer Dawn something. An apology? For shouting? For using her? She backed toward the door, saying instead, "I think I should go."

Dawn lifted disillusioned eyes. "Yes. I think you should."

CHAPTER SIXTEEN

Three days later, Annabel yawned and rearranged the cushions behind her head. "I still can't believe this," she told the gray-haired woman sitting opposite her.

"Fact is stranger than fiction, my dear," Violet Hazel pronounced. "How are you feeling this morning?"

"Terrific! I keep opening my eyes and wondering if I'm dead and this is just some kind of entrance exam for heaven." She lifted tentative fingers to explore the deep cut above her eyes. "That was some knock." Her head was throbbing and her vision was blurred, but she was alive! She glanced across at her companion. It was difficult to guess Violet Hazel's age — somewhere between sixty and eighty. Her face was creased and mobile, her eyes wonderfully blue.

Those eyes were the first thing Annabel had seen when she had lifted her head the day before. Then there was the voice, warm and rounded. "Well, good morning. Thanks for dropping by."

Annabel had decided immediately that she was in the presence of the Goddess herself. But to double-check, she'd asked where she was.

"You're on Solarim Atoll." Violet Hazel had informed her.

Solarim Atoll, an atoll so tiny it didn't even appear on most maps. And she'd found it. Annabel couldn't help but smile rather goofily at her good fortune.

Violet seemed amused. "You still congratulating yourself on cheating the Grim Reaper?"

"I can't help it. I really thought I was going to die. I was running out of fuel and I had no idea where I was ... I only saw this place minutes before I came down."

"Where were you headed?"

"Mitiaro."

"But that's at least six hundred miles northeast of here."

"It looks like I had instrument failure," Annabel explained. "My compass wasn't working and neither was my fuel gauge."

"I thought I might go and take a look at your plane this morning," Violet said. "Get her covered up."

Annabel's eyes started to sting. "I should come with you," she whispered. "But I don't think I can bear it." She pictured the Dominie, her sleek silver body mangled and smashed, skin torn to shreds. "The poor old thing." She sighed. "What an ignominious end for her."

"Hogwash," Violet said sternly. "She got you here, didn't she? And saved your life. If a machine has a spirit, hers will surely be rejoicing."

It was a bizarre notion, but curiously appealing all the same.

"The least you can do," Violet was telling her imperiously, "is return to thank her."

Annabel's eyes widened. Her companion was quite serious. She was an old eccentric woman, one part of Annabel rationalized. It would be polite to humor her. On the other hand, Annabel was weeping inside for the Dominie, that gallant little plane, condemned to a flightless future, to rot away on some unknown atoll.

Violet didn't wait for an answer. "C'mon. Let's go and see her," she said carefully, placing a capacious straw hat on Annabel's head. "Think you can walk a few yards at my pace?"

The Dominie was burrowed into the sand at the opposite end of the beach from Violet's cottage.

When they had cleared out all the surviving cargo, Annabel turned her attention to the instruments. They were still intact. She stared at the compass for a moment, glanced out at the sun, then called to Violet, "Which way is north?"

174

"That way." The white-haired woman pointed in the opposite direction from the compass, then climbed up to peer inside the plane. "Well, it wants to make a liar out of me, doesn't it?" Her eyes flicked from the instruments to Annabel's face, and with a purposeful air she retreated, appearing a moment later at the mangled nose of the plane. She wielded a pair of bolt cutters. "Come and see this," she announced after a couple of minutes.

Elbowing herself up, Annabel peered into the tangle of electronics. Violet had detached the compass from its mounting. Examining it, Annabel felt sick. There was a small square of metal clinging to its side. "It's a magnet," she said weakly.

"Otherwise known as sabotage," Violet whispered.

Leaning against the hangar doorway, Grace watched cigarette smoke curl into Bevan's thinning blond hair. "Well, I guess that's it," she said, wearily removing her flying gear. Although they had conducted their search at low altitude, it still got icy cold in the B-17.

Bevan handed her a lit cigarette. "Maybe," he said.

Grace glanced at him sharply. "You think she could still be alive?"

"No." He shook his head. "It's been a week."

"Smithy says the Dominie would have gone straight to the bottom," Grace commented.

"That's what the Air Accident Report concludes. Odd it doesn't say anything about those filed flight plans."

"How could they have made such a mistake?" Grace shook her head. "Someone wasn't doing his job. I can't understand why there's not some kind of inquiry."

"I gather the guy responsible has already resigned. They couldn't even locate him to get a statement."

"Wonderful." Grace stubbed out her cigarette. "He takes his final paycheck and gets drunk, Annabel rots at the bottom of the Pacific!"

"An' yer know somethin' else?" Smithy emerged from the hangar. "There warn't no medical 'mergency. Did wot yer said, guvnor. Checked wit' the wife's relatives. Never 'eard of no 'mergency."

"But what about that Red Cross parcel?" Grace said. "If there was no emergency on Mitiaro, why did the hospital send it?"

The old man's eyes began to water. "Aye, a curse on th'day I fetched the bleedin' thing," he muttered. "Darn fools."

Bevan drew on his cigarette. "They forgot to give it to Annabel, so you left her here, fetched the parcel and then returned?"

Smithy was shaking his head. "'Erself 'adn't arrived, so I nipped off an' picked it up meself."

"And Annabel wasn't here?" Bevan repeated.

"What are you saying?" Grace surveyed him with dawning comprehension.

"I'm saying I smell a rat," Bevan said mildly.

"Well gawd a'mighty! I jes' remembered somethin'." Rattling about in his overall pockets, Smithy extracted a pair of red-handled pliers and passed them across to Bevan. "Take a look at these, guvnor."

176

Bevan lifted an inquiring brow.

The wiry little man narrowed his eyes and spat to one side. "No' wot do yer suppose this 'ere tool is doin' 'ere, eh?"

"Can I speak with you?"

Bristling a little, Dawn glanced up from her Jackie Collins. She had barely spoken with Grace for the past three days, and that suited her fine. "What is it?" she said in a discouraging tone.

Beside her, Cody had removed her sunglasses. "Is there some news?"

Grace squatted, eyes grave with the burden of bearing the same ill tidings day after day. "I'm sorry," she said. It was a statement she'd been repeating often, of late. She had no map laid out to display search zones, no reports from the other craft, no spark of hope. She flicked a brief, expectant glance toward Dawn, asking, when Dawn remained uncooperative, "Could we talk in private?"

Cody had sagged back into her chair, her hands resting on the curling jacket of her paperback. Touching her arm in a gesture of comfort, Dawn said to Grace, "Later. Give me a call."

Grace's expression registered disbelief, rapidly followed by exasperation.

Before she had a chance to respond, Cody intervened. "It's okay, Dawn. I feel like some time on my own anyway."

Grudgingly, Dawn accompanied Grace along the walkway past the swimming pool to the lagoon. The beach shimmered with pale-bodied tourists, earnestly absorbing the tanning rays of the tropical sun. Negotiating a sea of sunscreen bottles, Dawn and Grace found a quiet spot toward Arorangi village.

Dawn sat, stiff-backed. "Well?" she said, avoiding Grace's eyes.

"The search is being scaled down," Grace replied heavily. "Bevan is going to continue flyovers for the next few days, but it's a long shot."

She sounded depressed. Fighting an urge to place an arm around Grace's shoulders, Dawn said, "Poor Cody."

Grace went on. "Cody's mom is arriving from New Zealand in an hour or so, and we've booked her here at the hotel. I figured we would fly back to Moon Island, this afternoon."

"What?" Dawn turned sharply. "What are you talking about?"

Grace sighed. "Look, I'm sorry we didn't discuss it with you, but we've been kind of busy. Someone has to run the island and Mrs. Marsters has managed for the last few days, but she's got a family."

"So I'm supposed to do it?" Dawn was incredulous. "I don't know the first thing about running a tourist resort."

"That's why I'm staying too."

The cheek. As if Grace Ramsay could manage any better. "Aren't you supposed to be back in New York?" Dawn reminded her damply.

"I've taken extra leave. Bevan and I have a few loose ends to tie up . . ." She trailed off, vague all of a sudden.

Grace and Bevan. It was sounding very cozy. Maybe there was another reason Grace was staying,

Dawn thought. Maybe Grace was one of those lesbians like Cody's ex — Margaret, the woman who'd lived with Cody for five years, then left her for a man. Now she was living on some ashram in southern India, wearing a sari and making flower garlands for her guru. According to her last letter, she was pregnant. She'd always wanted kids, Cody had said.

Frowning at Grace, Dawn said, "So stay on Rarotonga. I can run the island by myself "

Grace shook her head. "It's not practical, Dawn. You'd have to take the supplies around, either on horseback or driving the boat . . ."

"And you don't think I can!" Dawn raised her voice. "Because I have a limp, I'm some kind of incompetent — is that what you're saying?"

Grace sighed. "Be reasonable. Moon Island is a two-person job, and Cody's too depressed. Maybe we could put our differences aside for a few days and just get on with it. Surely it's the least we can do for Cody . . . and Annabel."

Dawn toyed with a handful of warm sand. "All right. So long as you stay out of my way, okay?"

"Okay," Grace agreed, and although her tone bordered on meekness, her eyes were anything but docile.

Meeting them, Dawn looked quickly away.

"It's hard to accept that someone wants to kill me," Annabel said. "I haven't *done* anything."

"Perhaps it's someone's idea of a joke," Violet said. "Nothing would surprise me."

"Violet! That's so cynical."

"My dear, at my age one cannot afford to harbor trite illusions about the nature of the human condition. The shock of disillusionment could prove fatal."

Annabel raised her hand to the ragged wound on her forehead. "I think we can rule out the joke idea. Maybe it's revenge, although I can't think of anyone I've wronged so badly they would want to kill me. And I would know, surely."

"I'm certain you would, my dear. Revenge is an act of powerful emotion. Most victims have some kind of relationship with their killers. When you think about it, suicide is just revenge turned inward. Such an intimate crime."

"Well, I definitely didn't plant that damned magnet myself," Annabel said. "And there's that Red Cross parcel. It was empty, remember."

"Indeed." Violet nodded thoughtfully. "So who would have something to gain by killing you? Who finds you a threat or an obstacle?"

Annabel hesitated. "It's crazy. But there is one person."

By the time Annabel had finished describing Robert Hausmann's bid to buy the island, his plans to use it for chemical dumping and his hints that the Cook Islands government might have been involved in insider trading, Violet was looking very satisfied.

"That's your man, Annabel. He's ruthless, greedy and unethical."

Annabel laughed. "Violet, you just described most of the so-called civilized world!"

"Why do you think I live out here?" Violet replied.

"How long have you been on Solarim?"

Violet gave that some thought. "Forty years," she pronounced. "Not all of it here on Solarim. I lived on Raro until the seventies."

Annabel's mind was spinning. If Violet had been in the Cook Islands for forty years, she must have known Aunt Annie. Yet she hadn't said anything when Annabel mentioned who she was and that she owned the island. Her heart started pounding.

"Did you ever visit Moon Island?"

"Several times." Violet's eyes creased with pleasure. "I think it's the most beautiful island in the whole Pacific. It's even lovelier than Aitutaki."

"I think so too." Suddenly Annabel felt like crying. She could almost see the moon suspended over Passion Bay, smell the late-night heaviness of frangipani and gardenia. She pictured Cody sitting alone on their veranda, waiting for her.

"There, there ..." Violet pulled her into the present with a pat on the hand. "You know," she said quietly, "you remind very much of someone I knew many years ago, Annabel. A child called Lucy Adams."

Annabel sat very still. "You knew ... Lucy?"

Violet promptly went inside the house and returned with a battered old photo album. "Oh, yes. Just look at this."

She singled out a fading photo, then another and another, until Annabel's eyes were so flooded she could no longer read the captions. Annie and Rebecca were gazing out of a sepia past, speaking to her heart after thirty silent years.

"It is you, isn't it?" Violet said.

Annabel could only nod dumbly. Her throat was too constricted for words.

"You were the most beautiful child I've ever seen. Rebecca was just mad over you. Look." She flipped the page and Annabel was staring at a woman with short black hair and brooding eyes. She was slouched against a tree trunk, wearing men's pants, one hand casually stuffed in a pocket, the other holding a tiny fair-haired child aloft. Lucy. Herself as a toddler.

"I remember that day still." Violet's voice shook slightly. "It was the day Rebecca left on the freighter to visit her family. And she never came back. Silly me." She dabbed at her eyes with an ancient handkerchief. "Now I'm getting all sentimental."

"Oh, Violet. This means so much to me. You have no idea . . ." Annabel was laughing and crying at the same time. "I can't believe this is happening. I must have been meant to come here. It was my destiny . . ."

"It most certainly wasn't," Violet reminded her. "It was attempted murder and we shall see the scoundrel responsible is brought to justice. Mark my words."

Annabel smiled. "That wasn't what I meant. But you know that, don't you. You're just teasing."

Violet lifted her eyebrows. "I'm very serious indeed, young woman. The freighter gets here tomorrow. It only comes once a month, you know, and if you're going to catch it, we've got work to do."

"Yes ma'am." Annabel immediately wiped her tears and sat up straighter in her chair.

Violet gave an approving nod. "But before we start, tell me, is your mother still alive?"

"Annie died three years ago. It's rather a long story, I'm afraid."

Violet's eyes crinkled. "Fortunately time is a blessing here, not a curse."

Annabel gave her a grateful smile. "Well, for a start, I didn't know I was Annie's daughter. Her sister Laura adopted me, you see, and renamed me Annabel Worth. After Rebecca died, Annie went back home to Boston and —"

"Oh this is going to be a long story," Violet broke in. "Why don't I fetch some tea and biscuits before it becomes truly gripping."

CHAPTER SEVENTEEN

"It's brilliant." Grace dropped a sheaf of neatly typed pages onto the table. "Right on the jugular."

"It's the very least the bastard deserves." Bevan passed a freshly lit cigarette to the thin, dark-haired man beside him.

Don Jarvis took a contemplative drag. "*Time* will go for it like sharks. Business ethics is hot right now."

"Where did you dredge up all that stuff?" Grace asked.

Don quirked an eyebrow. "A guy like Hausmann makes a few enemies on his way up."

"Do you think we've got enough for the police to go on?"

"If the government didn't pay their salaries, maybe."

"You mean they won't arrest him?" Grace was astounded.

"They can't. They've got way too much to lose. They're in shit to their eyeballs, sweetheart, and this place can't afford another Albert Henry."

"He was the Premier who got sacked for corruption, right?"

"It's not often Queen Elizabeth kicks ass." Don grinned. "But she did that time. Brought down the government."

"There must be some way . . ." Grace urged. "The bastards deserve everything they get. A woman is dead because they were looking to make a fast buck. We owe it to her."

"Grace, she wouldn't want it." Bevan stubbed out his cigarette. "She loved these islands. Have you any idea how much it would shame the local people if it went that far?"

"You're talking about murder!" Grace gasped. "And you're saying he's going to stay out of jail so that a bunch of corrupt bureaucrats can keep their jobs! That stinks."

"Politics does," Don said bluntly. He leafed through his article. "Look, I've turned up enough dirt on Hausmann to bury him. When this hits the press the IRS will be all over him like a biblical plague. The SEC will slap an injunction on the bastard so

185

fast he won't know which way is up. They've been on his tail for years. The guy will definitely serve time."

Grace cradled her head in her hands. They were right, of course. They couldn't prove a murder without either a plane or a body. And the last thing Annabel would want was to have the islands pilloried in the international press, thrown into political turmoil, their fragile economy shattered. But it was so unjust.

"It's not enough," she whispered, her face wet. No one ever really paid for the hurt they inflicted. Her guts were churning. There were four men roaming free out there who had stolen six weeks of her life and sentenced her to five years of emotional isolation.

"It won't bring her back, Grace." Bevan dropped an arm over her shoulders. "Revenge doesn't work that way."

Dawn wasn't at Villa Luna when Grace returned. Conscious of sharp disappointment, she prowled the house. Since their arrival on Moon Island four days before, communication with Dawn had been polite and distant. They slept in rooms at opposite ends of the Villa, ate meals together, and conducted the business of the resort with bright, impersonal diligence.

Dawn was always busy with something and gave the impression that interruption was not welcome. Most often she could be found in the garden, weeding and trimming. Sometimes she would be on the telephone chatting with a guest, and Grace would eavesdrop for a moment, then rattle about in the kitchen, aware of a petty kind of resentment.

It was not as if she had the time to be small-minded. Along with her responsibilities at the resort, she was involved in the investigation of Annabel's disappearance. Determined to follow up suspicions of foul play around Annabel's crash, Bevan had enlisted his lover, Don, a free-lance journalist, to sleuth around. The outcome had been even more shocking than they could have guessed.

It was all circumstantial of course. But a man in overalls was seen leaving the Dominie's hangar the afternoon Annabel left, and an Air Traffic Controller who had resigned was known to have departed for Auckland with unseemly haste and rather a lot of money. It also seemed clear that someone high in the ranks of officialdom was doing his best to obstruct inquiries around the accident — a classic cover-up job, Don had said.

Negotiating the track from Villa Luna to Passion Bay, Grace tried to convince herself that Don's exposé feature would do enough damage to compensate for what Hausmann had engineered. He would lose everything that really mattered to him — his reputation, his career, money. But all she could think about was Annabel, how she had been robbed of the happiness it had taken her so long to find, how much she had loved Moon Island and what that love had cost her.

Again the enormity of Hausmann's actions struck her. Environmental destruction was one thing, but murder? Reflecting uneasily on the ethics of both, she paused to disentangle herself from a sticky creeper overhanging the track. In some ways there was a logical progression. Numerous deaths had been caused through the disposal of toxic waste — was that murder? No, that was negative publicity. And Annabel? Why was that situation different? Because her death was more immediate, more personal? Because she was a wealthy, beautiful white woman?

Shoving her hands into her pockets, Grace crossed the hot sand to stand over the woman reclining on a huge, pink towel.

Dawn lifted her hat and blinked up into the sun. "Oh, it's you." She was wearing a very small bikini, doubtless a reluctant concession to Grace's intrusive presence at Villa Luna. It revealed more than it covered.

Kicking off her sandals, Grace lowered herself to the sand. She recognized Dawn's expression. Wariness and determined disinterest. Who could blame her, Grace thought, casting a wry, sideways glance at the younger woman. Dawn was apparently immersed again in her Jackie Collins.

After a few minutes' silence, she looked up. "Did you want something?"

"Your company, actually," Grace said.

Dawn shrugged. "Feel free." Flipping open the top of her sunscreen bottle, she methodically plastered her legs.

The scar tissue must be very sensitive, Grace guessed. She remembered seeing Dawn for the first time, her legs pale and wasted, scars knitting flesh torn by injuries too horrible to contemplate. How had it happened? What terror did she revisit alone at night? Grace stretched out her hand and touched a long white gash. "Tell me about the accident," she said.

Flinching, Dawn brushed off Grace's fingers the way she might an insect. "It was a car accident," she replied flatly.

"Do you know how it happened?"

"Look, do we have to discuss this? I was knocked out so I don't remember anything. One minute I was driving along, the next minute I was in hospital."

"Do you have nightmares?"

Dawn turned sharply, as though Grace were about to humilate her with some previously unsuspected sleeptime indiscretion. "No. But you do," she said.

Grace turned the stud in her ear. "Not any more. I had one last week and since then . . . nothing."

Dawn sat up, shaking the sand from her hair. "What makes you think that's it, that you won't have any more?"

Grace contemplated five years of waking in a sweat almost every night, of working so late she could barely keep her eyes open, in the hopes she might sleep the unbroken sleep of exhaustion. "Because I think dreams are messages and maybe they keep repeating until we're ready to hear them."

"And now you've heard yours?"

"I think so." Wrapping her arms around her knees, Grace leaned forward and stared out to sea. Was that how it worked? Was the conscious mind little more than a gatekeeper to the subconscious? Did dreams unlock doors to secrets housed within? She had concealed four faces there, the assailants she could not identify to the police. In protecting herself from the reality of her rape, she had protected her rapists too.

"Well, it sounds like a pretty complicated way of finding out something." Dawn was gathering her beach paraphernalia. She stood and brushed herself off. "Are you in for dinner?" Her expression gradually softened as she waited for an answer. "Grace," she ventured after a pause. "Are you okay?"

"I . . ." Grace shrugged helplessly, unable to rid her mind of those memories. She lifted a hand to her face, then stared at her wet fingers. A huge sob rose in her chest and suddenly she was keeling over, harsh retching sounds emitting from her own throat.

When Dawn's arms closed around her, she could offer no resistance. She simply sagged onto Dawn's shoulder, surrendering herself to a grief too profound to face alone any longer.

Several hours later, they were lying exactly where they'd crawled that afternoon, just under the covers. Grace had cried for what seemed an eternity. She had said nothing at all, just wept.

Dawn tilted her head to face the woman beside her.

"Hello," Grace murmured.

There was a gentleness in her face Dawn had never seen. And something else, something that seemed meant for her alone. Dawn stared, frightened that at any second the generosity would forsake that mouth, and cool, cynical Grace Ramsay would stare back at her.

If only she could freeze time, she thought, seize a

single magical moment before it fell prisoner to the inevitable disillusion. Love. It declared itself in siren promises, blazed like sunlight behind closed eyes, painted the air between them. Love. She had thought she would never know that feeling, thought she might fail to recognize it. She almost laughed.

Stroking Dawn's hair back from her face, Grace touched her cheek, cupping its baby fullness in her hand, and stretching her fingers to coil a soft honey-colored lock of hair. She saw with amazement that her fingers were shaking. Her whole body was shaking, in fact. The cynical Grace seemed oddly disengaged. You're going to make a fool of yourself, she clattered. But it was just noise and when her eyes locked with Dawn's there was silence, perfect and complete. Placing a hand to Dawn's chest, she felt the steady beat of her heart, took Dawn's hand and held it between her own breasts.

"We're in time," Dawn whispered.

"Can you forgive me?"

The baby-blue eyes widened. "For what?"

"For everything. I've treated you badly. I want to make it up to you."

Dawn was blushing. Grace lowered her head, kissed her slowly and tenderly on the mouth. Then she held her, frightened to speak, to move, in case she destroyed the fragile new bond between them.

CHAPTER EIGHTEEN

Dawn touched Cody's elbow. "How about a walk on Passion Bay?"

Cody shook her head, barely responding.

Dawn fidgeted. "Would you like something to eat?"

Another shake of the head.

"You really should. You're looking ill."

Cody shrugged listlessly. "I'm not hungry." Her shoulders sagged and she pushed her fingers back through her short dark hair. "I just can't believe it," she said softly.

"Cody . . ." Dawn stretched an impulsive arm, but Cody shied away.

Cody was disturbingly remote, avoiding touch, conversation. Her mother had thought it might be a good idea for her to return to Moon Island while arrangements were being made for Annabel's memorial service. Dawn wasn't so sure. All she seemed to do was stare out to sea.

People handle shock and grief in their own ways, Grace had said. But Dawn couldn't bear it. She was desperate to find some way to offer comfort. "I'll make us a cup of tea," she said and limped into the house.

She wished Grace were here. Grace seemed to know what to do when Cody forgot to go to bed or brush her hair. She'd been through something like it herself once, she said in an offhand tone that meant she didn't plan to say any more.

As Dawn arranged the teapot and cups on a tray she thought about Grace. Since that afternoon of weeping, she'd been so gentle and kind. They went walking and swimming together, talked for hours about Dawn's accident and her plans for the future. Grace helped with her exercise program, pushing her just that much harder than she might have pushed herself.

Yet Dawn felt she hardly knew her. Grace seldom talked about herself. She chatted easily about places she had been and things she had done, told amusing anecdotes about life in New York City. But she shied away from personal questions.

Dawn had extracted the information that she had a married sister in New Orleans and her English parents had retired to Miami Beach. Her family knew she was a lesbian and it didn't seem to be a problem. Grace had a small apartment somewhere called the East Village. She lived by herself. It was easier, she said without explaining why.

At times Dawn longed to ask her what it was she wasn't saying, but Grace always gave the impression of being so open and candid, and Dawn began to wonder if it was her imagination. Physically, it was the same. Grace was affectionate and approachable. They held hands and hugged like close friends. Yet Dawn felt unreasonably dissatisfied and irritated. Sometimes she just wanted the old flirtatious Grace back. She wanted to be thrown onto her bed. She wanted Grace to rip off her clothes and for them to make love for hours.

She couldn't understand why they weren't sleeping together. She had made it obvious enough that she wanted to, but Grace just didn't seem interested. Maybe she wasn't attracted to her that way anymore, Dawn thought miserably. Maybe it was because of Annabel.

She wished she had someone to talk to about it, but there was only Cody and under the circumstances, it was hardly an appropriate conversation topic. How could she think about sex at a time like this anyway? Full of self-reproach, she lifted the tray, balancing it carefully to compensate for her halting gait.

Cody was staring across Passion Bay with such attuned concentration, even Dawn found herself listening for the strangled hum of the Dominie, scanning the horizon for a glint of silver. Sometimes she simply forgot that Annabel would never come back again.

She offered a bone china cup to Cody, releasing a gasp of shock as it was knocked abruptly from her hand. "Cody!"

The other woman was already kneeling beside the shattered pieces, shoulders hunched. "I'm sorry," she whispered.

Dawn sprang down beside her. "It's okay. It doesn't matter."

"These are Annabel's favorites," Cody said, her tone hollow. She looked up at Dawn. "It's tomorrow, isn't it?" Her eyes were dark with pain.

The memorial service. Dawn nodded mutely.

"I just can't believe it," Cody whispered. Then she was on her feet, hurling the broken pieces down with a viciousness that sent the mynah birds fleeing from their hopeful sentinel along the veranda railing. "I can't believe it. I can't! I can't!" She was pacing the veranda, shaking her head. "Why," she suddenly shouted at Dawn. "Why did it have to be her? Of all the creeps out there who fucking deserve to die, why did they take her? Oh God, I can't bear it. She can't be dead. She's not dead!"

Dawn started to cry. She couldn't believe it either. There was a bizarre unreality about this whole experience. It felt like television. She almost expected to wake up and discover that none of this was really happening. She was not the Dawn Beaumont who had gone on holiday and fallen in love with a woman who didn't want her. Annabel hadn't crashed her plane. Cody wasn't acting like a madwoman.

"They haven't even found the plane. So how do they know she's dead?" Cody's pacing had turned to stomping. "The whole thing was a shambles. Why didn't they look for her when they got the distress call? It's their fault. And now she's gone. She's gone!" The final word was a wild sob, and then Cody was repeating the phrase over and over, weeping brokenly.

Annabel's memorial service was held in the gardens at Arorangi. It looked like everyone on Rarotonga was there, the devout islanders all dressed in their church finery. The early nineteenth-century missionaries responsible for such zeal had attempted to ban dancing, flowers and anything else that looked like fun. But the islanders weren't buying it, apparently feeling that the dour extremes of Protestant self-denial were best left to those fool enough to wear starched underclothes in the tropics.

Annabel's family was planning a ceremony back in Boston. They were on their way to Rarotonga to take Cody back with them. It wouldn't be anything like this, Dawn figured. There wouldn't be hundreds of people wearing flowers and crying noisily. There wouldn't be guitars and the biggest feast she had ever seen.

It was weird listening to a eulogy when there was no body to bury. Her attention strayed to Grace, then swung back to the preacher who was leading the service. A big silver-haired man in an ornate robe, he waved his arms a lot as he spoke. His sermon was in English and Maori, the two completely dissimilar languages fusing resonantly as he spoke.

Cody sat between Dawn and Bevan. Further along the pew were the Premier and various dignitaries. Obviously Annabel had been someone important around these parts. The preacher strode back and forth, pausing to direct comments to Cody.

Dawn was having difficulty following everything he said. He seemed to be talking about Moon Island and the various legends connected with it. Dawn supposed it was just superstition, but she was fascinated anyway.

To the early inhabitants of Rarotonga, Moon Island had been considered sacred to the Goddess of Fertility and to women. Legend had it that if men ever occupied the island, the Goddess would be angry, and no more children would be born to the Cook Islanders. This pronouncement seemed to generate considerable shuffling among the ranks of the dignitaries. The specter of infertility got the islanders pretty worked up too, given they weren't supposed to pay any heed to such idolatrous superstition.

"But we are blessed," the preacher declared, then added as something of an afterthought, "by the Lord." He waited for the devout to say amen. "We were sent two daughters to safeguard the island for our people."

Everyone clapped. Dawn was bewildered. This wasn't like any funeral she'd ever attended.

"But one daughter could only stay for a short time. And in that time she made many gifts to our people." This comment led to a flurry of fanning and sobbing. "Our daughter Annabel has gone," the preacher intoned. "May the Lord grant her eternal rest." Feverish amens. "But our daughter Cody

197

remains." Audible sighs of relief. "We weep with her at the loss of a loved one."

The crying was contagious. Dawn just couldn't stop herself. She blubbered noisily into her handkerchief, squeezing Grace's hand until her fingers went weak. Then a very strange thing happened. Cody got up as though she were in a trance and turned to face the congregation, her face startled, expectant.

An awed hush fell, and like the islanders, Dawn found herself craning in the direction Cody was staring, trying to see what it was she was seeing.

"Annabel?" Cody's whisper radiated into the hush.

The preacher tried to keep things in line. "Her spirit is with us."

Dawn's spine tingled. She could almost believe it.

Then a voice at the rear of the gathering said, "And so is her body." And accompanied by an old woman in very peculiar clothing, Annabel walked calmly through the throng and straight up to her lover, just in time to catch her as she fainted.

In the heady chaos that ensued, Dawn didn't know whether she was laughing or crying. There were people on their knees praying, others singing and clapping, the smell of food cooking. Annabel was all but buried in flowers and joked about being smothered to death. Cody was beside her looking flushed and dazed.

"It's a miracle," Dawn declared breathlessly and looked around for Grace in the milling crowd. She was nowhere to be seen. Jumping into the fray, Dawn elbowed her way over to Annabel and Cody. "Have you seen Grace?" she demanded as the two women caught hold of her.

Annabel scanned the faces around them. "She was here a minute ago talking with Bevan."

Dawn frowned. Grace was always off talking to Bevan. A man.

"She'll be back." Annabel smiled and gave her a squeeze. "Come with us and have something to eat."

Dawn's mouth watered at the prospect, but she wanted Grace. She wanted her now. "I'll just go and have a look for her."

As Dawn turned to leave, Annabel caught her arm. "I almost forgot. I've got something for you. It's been sweated on and bled on and very nearly died on." She produced a crumpled note. "Grace asked me to give this to you the day all this started. It seemed important, so I kept it for you."

Dawn unfolded the note and stared at its contents. A New York address and phone number and the words, *I lied. You do matter to me and that makes me scared. Please phone.*

Conscious she was starting to blush, Dawn stashed the folded paper in her pocket, kissed Annabel gratefully on the cheek, and hustled her way into the crowd.

Grace was nowhere to be found, and neither was Bevan. The more she hunted, the more frustrated she grew. Why weren't they here? This was Annabel's wake-turned-welcome-home party. What could they possibly be doing that was more important?

A nasty suspicion fluttered across her mind. Grace and Bevan? No. It couldn't be possible. They'd only been spending time together because they were involved in the search for Annabel. Well she was back now. So where the hell were they?

Dawn was fuming when she stumbled on Smithy, who was drinking beer. She tugged on his arm. "Have you seen Grace and Bevan?"

He looked startled, then faintly sheepish.

"It's important." Dawn was almost hopping from one foot to the other.

Smithy cleared his throat. "The guvnor did mention something about the hangar, Miss. But he said . . ."

Dawn didn't wait for him to finish. Bolting off in the direction of Main Street, she hitched a ride to the airport on the first minibus she spotted.

CHAPTER NINETEEN

"How long have you been with Don?" Grace asked as Bevan twisted segments of wire together with his pliers.

"Eight years."

"Don't you ever get sick of each other?"

"Quite the opposite."

Grace smiled wryly. She could believe it. She'd spent enough time around Don and Bevan to sense they were the male equivalent of Cody and Annabel. "You mean the novelty still hasn't worn off?"

"Novelty was never really the attraction. I think we'd both had enough of that for one lifetime."

Grace made a fuss of the knots she was working on. "You're quite a bit older than Don, aren't you?"

"About the same difference as you and Dawn." Bevan returned Grace's sharp look with an unrepentant grin. "You don't take too many chances, do you, Grace?"

"Only the kind that pay off."

"Life must be very predictable."

"I like it that way."

"Then I guess you'll be heading back home soon?"

She nodded stiffly. "In a couple of days' time."

Taking a few paces back, Bevan studied their masterpiece. "Well, what do you think?"

Grace fell in beside him, her gaze encompassing the B-17, festooned from nose to tail with tropical flowers and a huge pink bow twelve o'clock high. "I'll be honest with you Bevan. I think we could have saved ourselves a lot of trouble and just put a sack over its nose. Annabel would still kiss the propeller tips."

"Yeah, that's Annabel. No bullshit about her priorities."

"Why am I feeling got at all of a sudden?" Grace politely inquired.

Bevan lobbed a hard look in her direction. "What do you want, Grace? You want me to let you off the hook when you put yourself up there in the first place."

"Well, thanks. You're a real friend."

"Someone has to be."

Grace was stung to anger. "I gather this touching concern is all on account of Dawn Beaumont. I

202

suppose it wouldn't occur to anyone that maybe I'm not setting out to break her heart."

Bevan raised an eyebrow. "You weren't listening, were you?"

"I'm not used to a man telling me how to run my life."

"I'm not used to giving a damn if some mate of my boss's wants to shoot herself in the foot."

Grace's cheeks stung as if they'd been slapped. A *man* was calling her an emotional cripple. "Jesus, where do you couple-cultists get off?" she tossed at him. "Wise up, Bevan. Some of us aren't looking to be recruited."

"Sure, Grace. My mistake."

"Okay." Grace slammed her pliers onto the workbench. "Let's go get everyone. We're late for a party."

At Bevan's watchful silence, her anger faded. The two of them had been through some pretty rough times together during the last week or so, scouring the ocean for a glimpse of wreckage, trying to raise each others' spirits when all hope had gone. On impulse she tucked her arm into his. "Don't worry about me," she said. "It's nice of you, but I'll be okay, really."

Bevan met her eyes. "What about Dawn?"

"Yes, what about Dawn?" A small, cross voice carried across the airy hanger.

Grace caught her breath and turned slowly. Dawn was staring from her to Bevan, eyes full of accusation.

Bevan, yellow-gutted, wasted no time. "What say I go and pick up Annabel and Cody?"

"That's a good idea," Dawn told him, hands on

hips. Surveying him belligerently, she added, "And don't go getting any ideas about Grace. She's a lesbian."

"Dawn!" Grace stared after Bevan's retreating figure and tried to stifle her laughter. But it came out anyway, in a thin hysterical wheeze.

"Well, what's so funny?" Dawn demanded. "You go off with some man in the middle of the party and come out here to ... to ..."

"Dawn, Bevan's gay too."

Her jaw dropped, and she stared at Grace in disbelief.

"It's true. Don's his love."

Dawn's cheeks reddened, then she began to laugh. She finally noticed the bomber. "Grace, why has that plane got flowers and bows all over it?"

"Because it's a coming-home present for Annabel."

"From Bevan?"

"Sort of. He's giving her half of it. We just thought we'd pile on the glitz."

"Oh." Dawn's mouth formed a small round pucker. Grace wanted to kiss it.

"Annabel gave me this." The young woman's eyes dropped to a dog-eared note she was clutching. "I ... Well, it means a lot to me."

Grace couldn't bear to see her looking so dejected. "I couldn't just leave like that, Dawn," she said. "I thought I could, but fortunately there are limits even to my stupidity."

Staring at Dawn's upturned face, Grace felt dazzled, humbled. Her expression was so revealing — hopeful, a little indignant, way too vulnerable. Kissing her forehead, Grace slid her arms around Dawn's waist and drew her close. The silence between them stretched into one of those unexpected and glorious moments when happiness seemed there for the asking. Words fluttered precariously.

"Dawn," Grace began. "I ..."

A loud honking reverberated around the hangar and both women turned in startled dismay. Bevan's jeep blocked the doorway. Out of it piled half a dozen people: Bevan and Don, Smithy, Cody, the indomitable Violet, and a blindfolded Annabel.

She was making laughing complaints. "What is this? Plucked from the jaws of death and now I'm kidnapped!"

Bevan faced her toward the plane. Grace steered Dawn away as he removed the blindfold.

Annabel looked completely stunned. Flushing dark crimson, she stumbled toward the bomber. "It's a B-Seventeen" she whispered. Then she was smiling radiantly at Bevan. "How ..."

"I got lucky."

She stared up at the Vargas Girl painted on the fuselage and read, "*Lonesome Lady.*"

"Not anymore," Bevan commented.

Annabel was circling the nose, gazing up at the plexiglass. "I thought there were none of these left."

"She's one of a handful. There's a few still in service in the States. They use them for firebombing. And there's a couple in Europe. I saw *Sally B* while I was back home."

"Then where did *Lonesome Lady* come from?"

"One of my uncles rebuilt her after the war. She's been gathering dust on his farm ever since."

"And he's given her to you!"

Bevan nodded and tossed her a sheaf of papers. "Take a look."

Annabel was silent for a moment, flicking through them. "She's registered in both our names," she said huskily.

Beven offered his arm. "Want a tour of your plane?"

Smithy propped a ladder against the fuselage and opened the cockpit door.

Beaming, Annabel turned to Cody. "Isn't she wonderful!"

"Decent seats would be a bonus."

"Seats!" Smithy snorted. "Yer talkin' about a bomber, girl. C'mon." He cocked his head at Dawn, Grace and Don. "You lot can climb in 'er tail."

Dawn hung back a little. "You mean this plane was really in the war?"

"Got the flak marks to prove it." Smithy opened the rear door. "This old girl flew eight missions to Big B, an' she got 'ome every time."

"It dropped bombs on people?"

"Enemy targets," Smithy rasped.

Eyeing the gun turrets, Dawn felt even more squeamish.

Annabel stuck her head out the cockpit door. "We're taking her up, Smithy."

"C'mon." Grace lifted Dawn up to Cody, who was hanging out of the tail wearing a fleecy jacket. "I'll give Smithy a hand then I'll fight you for the ball turret."

They towed the B-17 out onto the tarmac. Grace chocked the wheels while Smithy radioed for clearance.

"Delay," he relayed to Annabel with an expressive scowl. "Some millionaire in 'is private jet."

"My God." Grace recognized the Argus logo. "It's Hausmann." She swung herself into the rear door and plunged along the B-17's tail to the radio room. "Hausmann's here," she told Don.

"Think you can get the asshole aboard?"

"Before I break his face, or after?"

Pushing past Dawn and Cody, Grace bailed out, shouted to Smithy to wait and pounded off across the tarmac.

"We'll all be arrested for this," Dawn muttered two hours later as Grace and Don frog-marched Robert Hausmann up the steps onto the veranda at Villa Luna.

"Nobody's going to be arrested," Annabel declared with conviction. "We've committed no crime."

"No crime!" Dawn exclaimed, following Annabel into the kitchen. "We've kidnapped a millionaire and threatened to push him out of a plane! We could end up in prison." Grace had lured Hausmann away from his entourage and assorted henchmen on the pretext of offering valuable new information. Don and Annabel had finished the job.

Annabel smiled. "Only if he tries to bring charges, and somehow I don't think he's about to do that."

"Well, why don't you go out there and make sure," Violet said. "I'll brew some tea." She glanced around. "Where do you keep your biscuits, dear?"

Dawn tossed her hands up impatiently. "This is madness. I'm catching the next flight out of here."

"Fine." There was laughter in Annabel's voice. "Are you going straight back to the airstrip or will you join us for tea first?"

Dawn headed for the door. "I'm going to see Grace," she declared.

Grace, Don, Bevan and Cody were gathered in a circle with Robert Hausmann at the center. He looked paler now than he had when he had first spotted Annabel. It would be just their luck if he popped off with a heart attack before they could get him back to Rarotonga, Dawn thought gloomily.

". . . so you could view this as an opportunity," Don was saying in a silky voice. "There's enough material in this article to fry your ass permanently. And an attempted murder rap won't do much for your credibility either."

"You can't prove a thing," Hausmann blustered.

"Oh sure," Grace said icily. "You knew Annabel would never sell so you backed right off. Then by some happy coincidence her plane went down. And before it was even reported, you'd already signed a contract with the Japanese to use the island for dumping."

"I can see the front cover of *Time* now," Don said. " 'Multinational Mob Tactics . . . Hausmann Plays Godfather in Pacific Dumping Scandal' . . . And you had it all worked out at this end too. A couple of malleable officials are paid to shut up, and the Government has a stake in keeping things quiet. You persuaded them to buy shares at a high. If the deal collapsed, the bottom would fall out of the stock and the Cooks would be bankrupted."

"I'm sure the Premier will be relieved to know Argus plans to buy back those shares at a premium," Grace added. "I don't know how you're going to explain it to the board, but that's your problem."

"Okay." Hausmann raised a hand. "I'm getting the picture loud and clear. What's your price?" He surveyed them with cynical self-assurance. "Two million and she gets to keep the island. We'll buy some other coconut kingdom. I really don't give a shit . . ."

"Then why not dump in your own back yard for a change, Mr. Hausmann?" Annabel emerged bearing a tray of teacups. Setting them down, she glanced around the small group. "I think that seems reasonable, don't you?"

Hausmann began, "What are you talking about —"

Grace cut him off. "I think she's saying maybe it's time companies like Argus started investing in alternative solutions to waste dumping. Like maybe the people who live here have a few rights too."

"So tell it to the French and the Japanese. Jesus, it's not my fucking problem. They want a service, we provide it. That's business."

"And murder?" Grace grabbed a handful of his shirt. "Is that business too? You're in big trouble, Hausmann. And for once you can't buy your way out." With an expression of disgust, she released him and turned to Annabel. "I think we're wasting our time. It's you he nearly killed. What do you want us to do with him, Annabel? Feed him to the sharks?"

Annabel was silent for a moment, then she mused, "Well, the Dominie was insured, and if it hadn't happened I might never have met Violet . . .

So I don't want him cast out to sea ... although I'm tempted. I guess what I really want is some kind of guarantee that Argus and companies like it will keep out of the Pacific."

"So maybe a public pledge from Argus that it will suspend all toxic dumping activities, a commitment to put a few million into researching alternatives like recycling, and maybe some significant donations to environmental agencies." Grace eyeballed Hausmann. "And you buy back that stock from the Cook Islands government and you make damned certain every Argus subsidiary minimizes waste production. In exchange we'll keep quiet and you'll stay out of prison."

Hausmann was shaking his head. "Impossible. We can't just get out of dumping. The Mexican contracts alone run for another ten years." Don was writing furiously.

"Okay. So you stay right out of the Pacific and you pressure other corporations to do the same," Grace said. "Argus is a major shareholder in a dozen manufacturers that I know are breaching their own countries' environmental protection statutes. I'll be watching for an improvement in their performance."

"You're serious." Hausmann looked incredulous. He shook his head. "Certifiable fucking tree-huggers."

"You finished drafting that agreement?" Grace asked Don.

"I'm not signing anything," Hausmann protested. "Our attorneys ..."

Ignoring him, Grace scanned the handwritten document then shoved it in front of him. "Give the man a pen," she said.

Dawn held her breath. She had never seen Grace

look more immovable. For a moment Hausmann stared at them, then with a shaking hand, he signed.

"Do you think we'll get away with it?" Dawn asked that evening on Rarotonga. They'd dumped Hausmann beside the Argus jet, waved Violet off on the Silk & Boyd freighter and were sitting in a conspicuous huddle around a table at the Banana Court.

"We have already." Don fluttered the contract Hausmann had signed. "This is witnessed."

Annabel frowned. "We did obtain his signature under duress."

"It was the least he deserved, surely," Grace remarked. "What's a black eye? I wanted to kill the bastard."

Dawn stared at Grace, scandalized at her brazen unconcern. "You'll lose your job," was all she could think to say.

Grace laughed, a low warm sound. "It's a bit late for that, Dawn. I've already resigned."

"You resigned!" Annabel remarked. "I confess I'm touched."

Grace looked wry. "Well, as much as I'd like to take credit where it's not due, the truth is, I was going to quit anyway."

"Tired of environmental sabotage?" Cody's tone fell slightly short of the lightness Dawn guessed she'd attempted.

Grace conceded the point with a slight ironic nod. "I guess deep down even I have a conscience, Cody."

"Well, that calls for a toast," Annabel said and paused a moment while they organized their drinks. "To conscience," she pronounced. "A saving grace in tragically short supply."

As they left the Banana Court, Dawn tugged at Grace's arm. "Have you really resigned?"

Grace took her hand and kissed the palm. "I guess I forgot to tell you."

Dawn halted in her tracks. "When? When did you decide that?"

Grace's eyes sparkled, her mouth twitched, then she started running.

"That's not fair!" Dawn hollered after her. "I can't run"

Grace put her hands on her hips and laughed. "So crawl!"

Outraged, Dawn flung her stick aside, negotiated her way through a throng of parked mopeds, and broke into a mutant form of running. "You wait, Grace Ramsay!" she bellowed.

And Grace did.

CHAPTER TWENTY

Grace reclined on a blanket beneath a group of rustling palms. Late afternoon was her favorite time on Hibiscus Bay. The heat of the day was fading from the grainy white sand, shadows deepened beneath the palm trees and the sky was bluer than the ocean.

Closing her eyes, Grace allowed her mind to wander. They were leaving tomorrow; she for the bite of a New York winter, Dawn to Sydney for Mardi Gras time. For a moment Grace allowed herself to wallow in envy. Sydney's gay community was large and thriving. She remembered her days living there as one endless party, from the Sleaze Ball to the Mardi Gras, the dances, the clubs and bars of Oxford Street. In East Sydney it was easy to forget there was a straight world at all. It was one of the best places in the world to be young, free and lesbian.

She imagined Dawn finding her feet there, imagined women picking her up, making love with her. She felt sick. Jealousy. Grace was all too aware of the contradictory feelings she had for Dawn. She'd been trying to sort them out ever since she'd decided to continue her stay on Rarotonga the day Annabel disappeared.

During that time she'd periodically contemplated a continuation of what had already happened. It would be so easy. Dawn had a crush on her. They could enjoy each other for a few months until the sexual tension dissipated. But she rejected the idea almost as soon as she considered it. She desired Dawn, yet it wasn't just sex she wanted, Grace realized. And it was way too late for a meaningless affair.

Sighing, she rolled onto her stomach and told herself she would get over it. Dawn wasn't her type. Grace thought about her warmth, the caring that her sometimes brash exterior disguised. She thought about her stamina, the gutsiness that had made her a champion swimmer before the accident and had got her through since then. She pictured Dawn's face, still bearing the last traces of childhood, eyes wide and curious, expression unguarded and at times painfully transparent.

She was far too young, Grace decided, and only

just coming out. It would be a disaster. Dawn would end up hurt and Grace would end up feeling like a jerk all over again. For a split second, Grace indulged herself in recalling Dawn's face suffused with passion, her mouth parted softly. She could almost feel Dawn naked beside her, trembling, responsive. She was Dawn's first lover. *It should have been someone else,* a small voice taunted her. It should have been a woman who really cared about her. At least in saying goodbye now, Dawn could go and find that woman.

She jerked abruptly as something cold and wet landed on her back. A sponge. Groping for it, she hurled it at the laughing woman standing over her.

"I was looking for you." Fending off the soggy missile, Dawn dropped down on the blanket beside Grace and set about removing her clothes.

God, she was beautiful. Grace squirmed as her companion prattled on happily about Annabel and Cody. Dawn tossed her shirt aside and rubbed sunblock across her breasts.

"My nipples are sore," she complained, examining them with a bemused expression.

Grace wanted to laugh hysterically. Hers were too, only not because they were sunburnt. She was becoming so aroused her breasts were aching.

"Look," Dawn said, pulling off her shorts and pointing proudly at her more damaged leg. "It's getting muscles."

Grace's gaze slid down the ragged scar; she noted the fuller thigh, the new hardening of the calf muscles. "It's great," she said, clearing her throat. She could hardly take her eyes off Dawn's thighs, the bright triangle of her bikini pants between them.

Dawn was so much less wary of showing her injuries now. Sometimes she seemed completely unconscious of them. She still took painkillers, but less often. Grace looked away, realizing she'd been staring.

Dawn must have noticed because her face was suddenly subdued. "Do my legs bother you, Grace?" she asked quietly. "Is that why you ... we ..." She sighed and slid down the blanket, closing the gap between them.

It wasn't the first time Dawn had alluded in a roundabout way to their recently platonic friendship. "No, of course not." Grace stroked the scarred flesh lightly, then permitted her arm to drift around Dawn's waist.

"Then why?" Dawn pleaded. "Why don't you want me any more ... was I no good or something?"

"No!" Grace denied sharply. "You were wonderful." Memories were flooding her senses — Dawn hot and wet, clinging to her, crying out. "I still want you," she admitted.

Dawn removed her sunglasses and stretched a hand to Grace's face, sliding her fingers into her hair. She brushed Grace's mouth with her own, whispering, "Then make love to me. Please."

Their kisses deepened. Dawn was touching Grace, tentatively, delicately exploring her. Unfastening clothing, Dawn slipped her hands across Grace's contours, drawing her closer until their bodies were perfectly aligned. They stared at each other, breathing hard, then without another word they got up and walked hand-in-hand into the jungle, leaving their blanket and clothing languishing beneath the tropical sun.

* * * * *

Dawn looked scared as they entered her bedroom, but she turned to Grace and moved into her waiting arms. Grace kissed her slowly then eased her onto the bed. For a long time they were still, holding each other. Then the heat of their bodies transformed to moisture and they slithered against each other, thighs intertwined, hands caressing, mouths tasting.

Grace felt wild laughter rise inside her at the sheer delight of Dawn's touch. But when her lips parted they met flesh and only a soft moan emerged.

She kissed and licked her way past damp perfect breasts, over Dawn's rounded belly, down to the silky blonde hair that divided her thighs. As her tongue traced its sensuous route, Dawn's legs closed around her head, imprisoning her. Grace turned her face to the pliant flesh, biting softly, then her mouth found the knit of scar tissue and she followed it tenderly along Dawn's leg. The younger woman stiffened at first then relaxed as Grace's hands took over from her mouth and she soothed the tenseness away with long even strokes.

"You're beautiful," Grace said, drawing back slightly to drink in the sight of Dawn's flushed cheeks, her eyes dark with arousal.

Dawn gasped with delight as Grace slid an arm beneath her, lifting her slightly and capturing her clitoris between fingers and thumb. Quivering, she rocked back onto her knees, twisting to face Grace.

They turned into each other's arms and Grace paused in her caresses, gasping when Dawn's teeth sank a gentle reminder into her shoulder. Her

217

breathing came in short harsh bursts, and her skin glowed pinkly. She murmured hoarse little pleas as Grace covered her neck in soft bites and licked the gathering moisture from between her breasts. Seizing Grace's hand, she guided it determinedly back and forth.

Grace slowly increased her pressure and with a sense of awe, felt Dawn's body tense. From somewhere deep in her throat a low sound emerged and the rhythm of their lovemaking altered sharply.

Shaking, Grace tightened her arm around Dawn's waist, feeling the building tension in Dawn's body and longing for its release. Dawn was finally gripped by a series of deep shudders. Grace collapsed against her, both of them laughing between wild kisses.

Grace couldn't remember changing positions, but suddenly Dawn was kneeling over her, gripping her shoulders. "I love you," she said, running her hands worshipfully across Grace's breasts. "Tell me what you want."

Grace took Dawn's hands, drew them to her mouth and kissed the fingers slowly and sensuously. There was a time when she could have answered that question in precise technical detail, but it felt like a thousand years ago now.

For a split second she felt defenseless and exposed, then she smiled and said, "You. I want you."

EPILOGUE

Three months later on Passion Bay, Cody announced, "It's a letter from Dawn. Want me to read out the best bits?"

Annabel peered out from beneath the brim of her hat. "It's not another description of the Clit Club is it? I think I'm getting old."

"No, they're in Sydney now. Grace got that Greenpeace job." Cody rustled papers. "Dawn came out to her folks. She says they're still praying."

"That's nice, dear."

"The cops never got those men Grace tried to

identify. But apparently she's started seeing a therapist. One in New York and one in Sydney."

"Remarkable."

"Dawn wants to borrow the B-Seventeen."

"Excuse me?"

"She's been taking flying lessons."

"What! "

"She wants to know how easy it is to skywrite."

"Dare I ask why?"

"For the Mardi Gras next year," Cody enthused. "She wants to paint a rainbow flag over Sydney."

A few of the publications of
THE NAIAD PRESS, INC.
P.O. Box 10543 • Tallahassee, Florida 32302
Phone (904) 539-5965
Mail orders welcome. Please include 15% postage.

SAVING GRACE by Jennifer Fulton. 240 pp. Adventure and
romantic entanglement.   ISBN 1-56280-051-5 $9.95

THE YEAR SEVEN by Molleen Zanger. 208 pp. Women surviving
in a new world.   ISBN 1-56280-034-5   9.95

CURIOUS WINE by Katherine V. Forrest. 176 pp. Tenth
Anniversary Edition. The most popular contemporary Lesbian
love story.   ISBN 1-56280-053-1   9.95

CHAUTAUQUA by Catherine Ennis. 192 pp. Exciting, romantic
adventure.   ISBN 1-56280-032-9   9.95

A PROPER BURIAL by Pat Welch. 192 pp. Third in the Helen
Black mystery series.   ISBN 1-56280-033-7   9.95

SILVERLAKE HEAT: A Novel of Suspense by Carol Schmidt.
240 pp. Rhonda is as hot as Laney's dreams.   ISBN 1-56280-031-0   9.95

LOVE, ZENA BETH by Diane Salvatore. 224 pp. The most talked
about lesbian novel of the nineties!   ISBN 1-56280-030-2   9.95

A DOORYARD FULL OF FLOWERS by Isabel Miller. 160 pp.
Stories incl. 2 sequels to *Patience and Sarah*.   ISBN 1-56280-029-9   9.95

MURDER BY TRADITION by Katherine V. Forrest. 288 pp. A
Kate Delafield Mystery. 4th in a series. ISBN 1-56280-002-7   9.95

THE EROTIC NAIAD edited by Katherine V. Forrest & Barbara Grier.
224 pp. Love stories by Naiad Press authors.   ISBN 1-56280-026-4   12.95

DEAD CERTAIN by Claire McNab. 224 pp. 5th Det. Insp. Carol
Ashton mystery.   ISBN 1-56280-027-2   9.95

CRAZY FOR LOVING by Jaye Maiman. 320 pp. 2nd Robin
Miller mystery.   ISBN 1-56280-025-6   9.95

STONEHURST by Barbara Johnson. 176 pp. Passionate regency
romance.   ISBN 1-56280-024-8   9.95

INTRODUCING AMANDA VALENTINE by Rose Beecham.
256 pp. An Amanda Valentine Mystery — 1st in a series.
                                          ISBN 1-56280-021-3   9.95

UNCERTAIN COMPANIONS by Robbi Sommers. 204 pp.
Steamy, erotic novel.   ISBN 1-56280-017-5   9.95

A TIGER'S HEART by Lauren W. Douglas. 240 pp. Fourth Caitlin
Reece Mystery. ISBN 1-56280-018-3   9.95

PAPERBACK ROMANCE by Karin Kallmaker. 256 pp. A
delicious romance. ISBN 1-56280-019-1   9.95

MORTON RIVER VALLEY by Lee Lynch. 304 pp. Lee Lynch at
her best! ISBN 1-56280-016-7   9.95

THE LAVENDER HOUSE MURDER by Nikki Baker. 224 pp. A
Virginia Kelly Mystery. Second in a series. ISBN 1-56280-012-4   9.95

PASSION BAY by Jennifer Fulton. 224 pp. Passionate romance,
virgin beaches, tropical skies. ISBN 1-56280-028-0   9.95

STICKS AND STONES by Jackie Calhoun. 208 pp. Contemporary
lesbian lives and loves. ISBN 1-56280-020-5   9.95

DELIA IRONFOOT by Jeane Harris. 192 pp. Adventure for Delia
and Beth in the Utah mountains. ISBN 1-56280-014-0   9.95

UNDER THE SOUTHERN CROSS by Claire McNab. 192 pp.
Romantic nights Down Under. ISBN 1-56280-011-6   9.95

RIVERFINGER WOMEN by Elana Nachman/Dykewomon.
208 pp. Classic Lesbian/feminist novel. ISBN 1-56280-013-2   8.95

A CERTAIN DISCONTENT by Cleve Boutell. 240 pp. A unique
coterie of women. ISBN 1-56280-009-4   9.95

GRASSY FLATS by Penny Hayes. 256 pp. Lesbian romance in
the '30s. ISBN 1-56280-010-8   9.95

A SINGULAR SPY by Amanda K. Williams. 192 pp. 3rd spy novel
featuring Lesbian agent Madison McGuire. ISBN 1-56280-008-6   8.95

THE END OF APRIL by Penny Sumner. 240 pp. A Victoria Cross
Mystery. First in a series. ISBN 1-56280-007-8   8.95

A FLIGHT OF ANGELS by Sarah Aldridge. 240 pp. Romance set at
the National Gallery of Art ISBN 1-56280-001-9   9.95

HOUSTON TOWN by Deborah Powell. 208 pp. A Hollis Carpenter
mystery. Second in a series. ISBN 1-56280-006-X   8.95

KISS AND TELL by Robbi Sommers. 192 pp. Scorching stories by
the author of *Pleasures*. ISBN 1-56280-005-1   9.95

STILL WATERS by Pat Welch. 208 pp. Second in the Helen
Black mystery series. ISBN 0-941483-97-5   9.95

MURDER IS GERMANE by Karen Saum. 224 pp. The 2nd
Brigid Donovan mystery. ISBN 0-941483-98-3   8.95

TO LOVE AGAIN by Evelyn Kennedy. 208 pp. Wildly
romantic love story. ISBN 0-941483-85-1   9.95

IN THE GAME by Nikki Baker. 192 pp. A Virginia Kelly
mystery. First in a series. ISBN 01-56280-004-3   9.95

AVALON by Mary Jane Jones. 256 pp. A Lesbian Arthurian
romance. ISBN 0-941483-96-7   9.95

STRANDED by Camarin Grae. 320 pp. Entertaining, riveting
adventure.   ISBN 0-941483-99-1   9.95

THE DAUGHTERS OF ARTEMIS by Lauren Wright Douglas.
240 pp. Third Caitlin Reece mystery.   ISBN 0-941483-95-9   9.95

CLEARWATER by Catherine Ennis. 176 pp. Romantic secrets
of a small Louisiana town.   ISBN 0-941483-65-7   8.95

THE HALLELUJAH MURDERS by Dorothy Tell. 176 pp.
Second Poppy Dillworth mystery.   ISBN 0-941483-88-6   8.95

ZETA BASE by Judith Alguire. 208 pp. Lesbian triangle
on a future Earth.   ISBN 0-941483-94-0   9.95

SECOND CHANCE by Jackie Calhoun. 256 pp. Contemporary
Lesbian lives and loves.   ISBN 0-941483-93-2   9.95

BENEDICTION by Diane Salvatore. 272 pp. Striking,
contemporary romantic novel.   ISBN 0-941483-90-8   9.95

CALLING RAIN by Karen Marie Christa Minns. 240 pp.
Spellbinding, erotic love story   ISBN 0-941483-87-8   9.95

BLACK IRIS by Jeane Harris. 192 pp. Caroline's hidden past . . .
                                        ISBN 0-941483-68-1   8.95

TOUCHWOOD by Karin Kallmaker. 240 pp. Loving, May/
December romance.   ISBN 0-941483-76-2   9.95

BAYOU CITY SECRETS by Deborah Powell. 224 pp. A Hollis
Carpenter mystery. First in a series.   ISBN 0-941483-91-6   9.95

COP OUT by Claire McNab. 208 pp. 4th Det. Insp. Carol Ashton
mystery.   ISBN 0-941483-84-3   9.95

LODESTAR by Phyllis Horn. 224 pp. Romantic, fast-moving
adventure.   ISBN 0-941483-83-5   8.95

THE BEVERLY MALIBU by Katherine V. Forrest. 288 pp. A
Kate Delafield Mystery. 3rd in a series.   ISBN 0-941483-48-7   9.95

THAT OLD STUDEBAKER by Lee Lynch. 272 pp. Andy's affair
with Regina and her attachment to her beloved car.
                                        ISBN 0-941483-82-7   9.95

PASSION'S LEGACY by Lori Paige. 224 pp. Sarah is swept into
the arms of Augusta Pym in this delightful historical romance.
                                        ISBN 0-941483-81-9   8.95

THE PROVIDENCE FILE by Amanda Kyle Williams. 256 pp.
Second espionage thriller featuring lesbian agent Madison McGuire
                                        ISBN 0-941483-92-4   8.95

I LEFT MY HEART by Jaye Maiman. 320 pp. A Robin Miller
Mystery. First in a series.   ISBN 0-941483-72-X   9.95

THE PRICE OF SALT by Patricia Highsmith (writing as Claire
Morgan). 288 pp. Classic lesbian novel, first issued in 1952 . . .
acknowledged by its author under her own, very famous, name.
                                        ISBN 1-56280-003-5   9.95

SIDE BY SIDE by Isabel Miller. 256 pp. From beloved author of
Patience and Sarah.   ISBN 0-941483-77-0   9.95

SOUTHBOUND by Sheila Ortiz Taylor. 240 pp. Hilarious sequel
to *Faultline.*   ISBN 0-941483-78-9   8.95

STAYING POWER: LONG TERM LESBIAN COUPLES
by Susan E. Johnson. 352 pp. Joys of coupledom.
                                         ISBN 0-941-483-75-4   12.95

SLICK by Camarin Grae. 304 pp. Exotic, erotic adventure.
                                         ISBN 0-941483-74-6   9.95

NINTH LIFE by Lauren Wright Douglas. 256 pp. A Caitlin
Reece mystery. 2nd in a series.   ISBN 0-941483-50-9   8.95

PLAYERS by Robbi Sommers. 192 pp. Sizzling, erotic novel.
                                         ISBN 0-941483-73-8   9.95

MURDER AT RED ROOK RANCH by Dorothy Tell. 224 pp.
First Poppy Dillworth adventure.   ISBN 0-941483-80-0   8.95

LESBIAN SURVIVAL MANUAL by Rhonda Dicksion.
112 pp. Cartoons!   ISBN 0-941483-71-1   8.95

A ROOM FULL OF WOMEN by Elisabeth Nonas. 256 pp.
Contemporary Lesbian lives.   ISBN 0-941483-69-X   9.95

MURDER IS RELATIVE by Karen Saum. 256 pp. The first
Brigid Donovan mystery.   ISBN 0-941483-70-3   8.95

PRIORITIES by Lynda Lyons 288 pp. Science fiction with
a twist.   ISBN 0-941483-66-5   8.95

THEME FOR DIVERSE INSTRUMENTS by Jane Rule. 208
pp. Powerful romantic lesbian stories.   ISBN 0-941483-63-0   8.95

LESBIAN QUERIES by Hertz & Ertman. 112 pp. The questions
you were too embarrassed to ask.   ISBN 0-941483-67-3   8.95

CLUB 12 by Amanda Kyle Williams. 288 pp. Espionage thriller
featuring a lesbian agent!   ISBN 0-941483-64-9   8.95

DEATH DOWN UNDER by Claire McNab. 240 pp. 3rd Det.
Insp. Carol Ashton mystery.   ISBN 0-941483-39-8   9.95

MONTANA FEATHERS by Penny Hayes. 256 pp. Vivian and
Elizabeth find love in frontier Montana. ISBN 0-941483-61-4   8.95

CHESAPEAKE PROJECT by Phyllis Horn. 304 pp. Jessie &
Meredith in perilous adventure.   ISBN 0-941483-58-4   8.95

LIFESTYLES by Jackie Calhoun. 224 pp. Contemporary Lesbian
lives and loves.   ISBN 0-941483-57-6   9.95

VIRAGO by Karen Marie Christa Minns. 208 pp. Darsen has
chosen Ginny.   ISBN 0-941483-56-8   8.95

WILDERNESS TREK by Dorothy Tell. 192 pp. Six women on
vacation learning ''new'' skills.   ISBN 0-941483-60-6   8.95

MURDER BY THE BOOK by Pat Welch. 256 pp. A Helen
Black Mystery. First in a series.　　　ISBN 0-941483-59-2　　9.95

BERRIGAN by Vicki P. McConnell. 176 pp. Youthful Lesbian —
romantic, idealistic Berrigan.　　　ISBN 0-941483-55-X　　8.95

LESBIANS IN GERMANY by Lillian Faderman & B. Eriksson.
128 pp. Fiction, poetry, essays.　　　ISBN 0-941483-62-2　　8.95

THERE'S SOMETHING I'VE BEEN MEANING TO TELL
YOU Ed. by Loralee MacPike. 288 pp. Gay men and lesbians
coming out to their children.　　　ISBN 0-941483-44-4　　9.95

LIFTING BELLY by Gertrude Stein. Ed. by Rebecca Mark. 104
pp. Erotic poetry.　　　ISBN 0-941483-51-7　　8.95

ROSE PENSKI by Roz Perry. 192 pp. Adult lovers in a long-term
relationship.　　　ISBN 0-941483-37-1　　8.95

AFTER THE FIRE by Jane Rule. 256 pp. Warm, human novel
by this incomparable author.　　　ISBN 0-941483-45-2　　8.95

SUE SLATE, PRIVATE EYE by Lee Lynch. 176 pp. The gay
folk of Peacock Alley are *all cats*.　　　ISBN 0-941483-52-5　　8.95

CHRIS by Randy Salem. 224 pp. Golden oldie. Handsome Chris
and her adventures.　　　ISBN 0-941483-42-8　　8.95

THREE WOMEN by March Hastings. 232 pp. Golden oldie. A
triangle among wealthy sophisticates.　　　ISBN 0-941483-43-6　　8.95

RICE AND BEANS by Valeria Taylor. 232 pp. Love and
romance on poverty row.　　　ISBN 0-941483-41-X　　8.95

PLEASURES by Robbi Sommers. 204 pp. Unprecedented
eroticism.　　　ISBN 0-941483-49-5　　8.95

EDGEWISE by Camarin Grae. 372 pp. Spellbinding
adventure.　　　ISBN 0-941483-19-3　　9.95

FATAL REUNION by Claire McNab. 224 pp. 2nd Det. Inspec.
Carol Ashton mystery.　　　ISBN 0-941483-40-1　　8.95

KEEP TO ME STRANGER by Sarah Aldridge. 372 pp. Romance
set in a department store dynasty.　　　ISBN 0-941483-38-X　　9.95

HEARTSCAPE by Sue Gambill. 204 pp. American lesbian in
Portugal.　　　ISBN 0-941483-33-9　　8.95

IN THE BLOOD by Lauren Wright Douglas. 252 pp. Lesbian
science fiction adventure fantasy　　　ISBN 0-941483-22-3　　8.95

THE BEE'S KISS by Shirley Verel. 216 pp. Delicate, delicious
romance.　　　ISBN 0-941483-36-3　　8.95

RAGING MOTHER MOUNTAIN by Pat Emmerson. 264 pp.
Furosa Firechild's adventures in Wonderland.　ISBN 0-941483-35-5　　8.95

IN EVERY PORT by Karin Kallmaker. 228 pp. Jessica's sexy,
adventuresome travels.　　　ISBN 0-941483-37-7　　9.95

OF LOVE AND GLORY by Evelyn Kennedy. 192 pp. Exciting
WWII romance.   ISBN 0-941483-32-0   8.95

CLICKING STONES by Nancy Tyler Glenn. 288 pp. Love
transcending time.   ISBN 0-941483-31-2   9.95

SURVIVING SISTERS by Gail Pass. 252 pp. Powerful love
story.   ISBN 0-941483-16-9   8.95

SOUTH OF THE LINE by Catherine Ennis. 216 pp. Civil War
adventure.   ISBN 0-941483-29-0   8.95

WOMAN PLUS WOMAN by Dolores Klaich. 300 pp. Supurb
Lesbian overview.   ISBN 0-941483-28-2   9.95

SLOW DANCING AT MISS POLLY'S by Sheila Ortiz Taylor.
96 pp. Lesbian Poetry   ISBN 0-941483-30-4   7.95

DOUBLE DAUGHTER by Vicki P. McConnell. 216 pp. A Nyla
Wade Mystery, third in the series.   ISBN 0-941483-26-6   8.95

HEAVY GILT by Delores Klaich. 192 pp. Lesbian detective/
disappearing homophobes/upper class gay society.
                                     ISBN 0-941483-25-8   8.95

THE FINER GRAIN by Denise Ohio. 216 pp. Brilliant young
college lesbian novel.   ISBN 0-941483-11-8   8.95

THE AMAZON TRAIL by Lee Lynch. 216 pp. Life, travel & lore
of famous lesbian author.   ISBN 0-941483-27-4   8.95

HIGH CONTRAST by Jessie Lattimore. 264 pp. Women of the
Crystal Palace.   ISBN 0-941483-17-7   8.95

OCTOBER OBSESSION by Meredith More. Josie's rich, secret
Lesbian life.   ISBN 0-941483-18-5   8.95

LESBIAN CROSSROADS by Ruth Baetz. 276 pp. Contemporary
Lesbian lives.   ISBN 0-941483-21-5   9.95

BEFORE STONEWALL: THE MAKING OF A GAY AND
LESBIAN COMMUNITY by Andrea Weiss & Greta Schiller.
96 pp., 25 illus.   ISBN 0-941483-20-7   7.95

WE WALK THE BACK OF THE TIGER by Patricia A. Murphy.
192 pp. Romantic Lesbian novel/beginning women's movement.
                                     ISBN 0-941483-13-4   8.95

SUNDAY'S CHILD by Joyce Bright. 216 pp. Lesbian athletics, at
last the novel about sports.   ISBN 0-941483-12-6   8.95

OSTEN'S BAY by Zenobia N. Vole. 204 pp. Sizzling adventure
romance set on Bonaire.   ISBN 0-941483-15-0   8.95

LESSONS IN MURDER by Claire McNab. 216 pp. 1st Det. Inspec.
Carol Ashton mystery — erotic tension!.   ISBN 0-941483-14-2   8.95

YELLOWTHROAT by Penny Hayes. 240 pp. Margarita, bandit,
kidnaps Julia.   ISBN 0-941483-10-X   8.95

SAPPHISTRY: THE BOOK OF LESBIAN SEXUALITY by
Pat Califia. 3d edition, revised. 208 pp.   ISBN 0-941483-24-X   10.95

CHERISHED LOVE by Evelyn Kennedy. 192 pp. Erotic
Lesbian love story.   ISBN 0-941483-08-8   9.95

LAST SEPTEMBER by Helen R. Hull. 208 pp. Six stories & a
glorious novella.   ISBN 0-941483-09-6   8.95

THE SECRET IN THE BIRD by Camarin Grae. 312 pp. Striking,
psychological suspense novel.   ISBN 0-941483-05-3   8.95

TO THE LIGHTNING by Catherine Ennis. 208 pp. Romantic
Lesbian 'Robinson Crusoe' adventure.   ISBN 0-941483-06-1   8.95

THE OTHER SIDE OF VENUS by Shirley Verel. 224 pp.
Luminous, romantic love story.   ISBN 0-941483-07-X   8.95

DREAMS AND SWORDS by Katherine V. Forrest. 192 pp.
Romantic, erotic, imaginative stories.   ISBN 0-941483-03-7   8.95

MEMORY BOARD by Jane Rule. 336 pp. Memorable novel
about an aging Lesbian couple.   ISBN 0-941483-02-9   9.95

THE ALWAYS ANONYMOUS BEAST by Lauren Wright
Douglas. 224 pp. A Caitlin Reece mystery. First in a series.
                                               ISBN 0-941483-04-5   8.95

SEARCHING FOR SPRING by Patricia A. Murphy. 224 pp.
Novel about the recovery of love.   ISBN 0-941483-00-2   8.95

DUSTY'S QUEEN OF HEARTS DINER by Lee Lynch. 240 pp.
Romantic blue-collar novel.   ISBN 0-941483-01-0   8.95

PARENTS MATTER by Ann Muller. 240 pp. Parents'
relationships with Lesbian daughters and gay sons.
                                               ISBN 0-930044-91-6   9.95

THE PEARLS by Shelley Smith. 176 pp. Passion and fun in
the Caribbean sun.   ISBN 0-930044-93-2   7.95

MAGDALENA by Sarah Aldridge. 352 pp. Epic Lesbian novel
set on three continents.   ISBN 0-930044-99-1   8.95

THE BLACK AND WHITE OF IT by Ann Allen Shockley.
144 pp. Short stories.   ISBN 0-930044-96-7   7.95

SAY JESUS AND COME TO ME by Ann Allen Shockley. 288
pp. Contemporary romance.   ISBN 0-930044-98-3   8.95

LOVING HER by Ann Allen Shockley. 192 pp. Romantic love
story.   ISBN 0-930044-97-5   7.95

MURDER AT THE NIGHTWOOD BAR by Katherine V.
Forrest. 240 pp. A Kate Delafield mystery. Second in a series.
                                               ISBN 0-930044-92-4   9.95

ZOE'S BOOK by Gail Pass. 224 pp. Passionate, obsessive love
story.   ISBN 0-930044-95-9   7.95

WINGED DANCER by Camarin Grae. 228 pp. Erotic Lesbian
adventure story.   ISBN 0-930044-88-6   8.95

PAZ by Camarin Grae. 336 pp. Romantic Lesbian adventurer
with the power to change the world.   ISBN 0-930044-89-4   8.95

SOUL SNATCHER by Camarin Grae. 224 pp. A puzzle, an
adventure, a mystery — Lesbian romance.   ISBN 0-930044-90-8   8.95

THE LOVE OF GOOD WOMEN by Isabel Miller. 224 pp.
Long-awaited new novel by the author of the beloved *Patience*
and Sarah.   ISBN 0-930044-81-9   8.95

THE HOUSE AT PELHAM FALLS by Brenda Weathers. 240
pp. Suspenseful Lesbian ghost story.   ISBN 0-930044-79-7   7.95

HOME IN YOUR HANDS by Lee Lynch. 240 pp. More stories
from the author of *Old Dyke Tales*.   ISBN 0-930044-80-0   7.95

EACH HAND A MAP by Anita Skeen. 112 pp. Real-life poems
that touch us all.   ISBN 0-930044-82-7   6.95

SURPLUS by Sylvia Stevenson. 342 pp. A classic early Lesbian
novel.   ISBN 0-930044-78-9   7.95

PEMBROKE PARK by Michelle Martin. 256 pp. Derring-do
and daring romance in Regency England.   ISBN 0-930044-77-0   7.95

THE LONG TRAIL by Penny Hayes. 248 pp. Vivid adventures
of two women in love in the old west.   ISBN 0-930044-76-2   8.95

HORIZON OF THE HEART by Shelley Smith. 192 pp. Hot
romance in summertime New England.   ISBN 0-930044-75-4   7.95

AN EMERGENCE OF GREEN by Katherine V. Forrest. 288
pp. Powerful novel of sexual discovery.   ISBN 0-930044-69-X   9.95

THE LESBIAN PERIODICALS INDEX edited by Claire
Potter. 432 pp. Author & subject index.   ISBN 0-930044-74-6   29.95

DESERT OF THE HEART by Jane Rule. 224 pp. A classic;
basis for the movie *Desert Hearts*.   ISBN 0-930044-73-8   9.95

SPRING FORWARD/FALL BACK by Sheila Ortiz Taylor.
288 pp. Literary novel of timeless love.   ISBN 0-930044-70-3   7.95

FOR KEEPS by Elisabeth Nonas. 144 pp. Contemporary novel
about losing and finding love.   ISBN 0-930044-71-1   7.95

TORCHLIGHT TO VALHALLA by Gale Wilhelm. 128 pp.
Classic novel by a great Lesbian writer.   ISBN 0-930044-68-1   7.95

LESBIAN NUNS: BREAKING SILENCE edited by Rosemary
Curb and Nancy Manahan. 432 pp. Unprecedented autobiographies
of religious life.   ISBN 0-930044-62-2   9.95

THE SWASHBUCKLER by Lee Lynch. 288 pp. Colorful novel
set in Greenwich Village in the sixties.   ISBN 0-930044-66-5   8.95

MISFORTUNE'S FRIEND by Sarah Aldridge. 320 pp. Historical Lesbian novel set on two continents.   ISBN 0-930044-67-3   7.95

A STUDIO OF ONE'S OWN by Ann Stokes. Edited by
Dolores Klaich. 128 pp. Autobiography. ISBN 0-930044-64-9 7.95

SEX VARIANT WOMEN IN LITERATURE by Jeannette
Howard Foster. 448 pp. Literary history. ISBN 0-930044-65-7 8.95

A HOT-EYED MODERATE by Jane Rule. 252 pp. Hard-hitting
essays on gay life; writing; art. ISBN 0-930044-57-6 7.95

INLAND PASSAGE AND OTHER STORIES by Jane Rule.
288 pp. Wide-ranging new collection. ISBN 0-930044-56-8 7.95

WE TOO ARE DRIFTING by Gale Wilhelm. 128 pp. Timeless
Lesbian novel, a masterpiece. ISBN 0-930044-61-4 6.95

AMATEUR CITY by Katherine V. Forrest. 224 pp. A Kate
Delafield mystery. First in a series. ISBN 0-930044-55-X 9.95

THE SOPHIE HOROWITZ STORY by Sarah Schulman. 176
pp. Engaging novel of madcap intrigue. ISBN 0-930044-54-1 7.95

THE YOUNG IN ONE ANOTHER'S ARMS by Jane Rule. 224 pp. Classic
Jane Rule. ISBN 0-930044-53-3 9.95

OLD DYKE TALES by Lee Lynch. 224 pp. Extraordinary
stories of our diverse Lesbian lives. ISBN 0-930044-51-7 8.95

DAUGHTERS OF A CORAL DAWN by Katherine V. Forrest.
240 pp. Novel set in a Lesbian new world. ISBN 0-930044-50-9 8.95

AGAINST THE SEASON by Jane Rule. 224 pp. Luminous,
complex novel of interrelationships. ISBN 0-930044-48-7 8.95

LOVERS IN THE PRESENT AFTERNOON by Kathleen
Fleming. 288 pp. A novel about recovery and growth.
ISBN 0-930044-46-0 8.95

TOOTHPICK HOUSE by Lee Lynch. 264 pp. Love between
two Lesbians of different classes. ISBN 0-930044-45-2 7.95

MADAME AURORA by Sarah Aldridge. 256 pp. Historical
novel featuring a charismatic ''seer.'' ISBN 0-930044-44-4 7.95

BLACK LESBIAN IN WHITE AMERICA by Anita Cornwell.
141 pp. Stories, essays, autobiography. ISBN 0-930044-41-X 7.95

CONTRACT WITH THE WORLD by Jane Rule. 340 pp.
Powerful, panoramic novel of gay life. ISBN 0-930044-28-2 9.95

MRS. PORTER'S LETTER by Vicki P. McConnell. 224 pp.
The first Nyla Wade mystery. ISBN 0-930044-29-0 7.95

TO THE CLEVELAND STATION by Carol Anne Douglas.
192 pp. Interracial Lesbian love story. ISBN 0-930044-27-4 6.95

THE NESTING PLACE by Sarah Aldridge. 224 pp. A
three-woman triangle — love conquers all! ISBN 0-930044-26-6 7.95

THIS IS NOT FOR YOU by Jane Rule. 284 pp. A letter to a
beloved is also an intricate novel. ISBN 0-930044-25-8 8.95

FAULTLINE by Sheila Ortiz Taylor. 140 pp. Warm, funny,
literate story of a startling family.   ISBN 0-930044-24-X   6.95

ANNA'S COUNTRY by Elizabeth Lang. 208 pp. A woman
finds her Lesbian identity.   ISBN 0-930044-19-3   8.95

PRISM by Valerie Taylor. 158 pp. A love affair between two
women in their sixties.   ISBN 0-930044-18-5   6.95

OUTLANDER by Jane Rule. 207 pp. Short stories and essays
by one of our finest writers.   ISBN 0-930044-17-7   8.95

ALL TRUE LOVERS by Sarah Aldridge. 292 pp. Romantic
novel set in the 1930s and 1940s.   ISBN 0-930044-10-X   8.95

A WOMAN APPEARED TO ME by Renee Vivien. 65 pp. A
classic; translated by Jeannette H. Foster.   ISBN 0-930044-06-1   5.00

CYTHEREA'S BREATH by Sarah Aldridge. 240 pp. Romantic
novel about women's entrance into medicine.
                                               ISBN 0-930044-02-9   6.95

TOTTIE by Sarah Aldridge. 181 pp. Lesbian romance in the
turmoil of the sixties.   ISBN 0-930044-01-0   6.95

THE LATECOMER by Sarah Aldridge. 107 pp. A delicate love
story.   ISBN 0-930044-00-2   6.95

ODD GIRL OUT by Ann Bannon.   ISBN 0-930044-83-5   5.95
I AM A WOMAN 84-3; WOMEN IN THE SHADOWS 85-1;   each
JOURNEY TO A WOMAN 86-X; BEEBO BRINKER 87-8. Golden
oldies about life in Greenwich Village.

JOURNEY TO FULFILLMENT, A WORLD WITHOUT MEN, and   3.95
RETURN TO LESBOS. All by Valerie Taylor   each

These are just a few of the many Naiad Press titles — we are the oldest and
largest lesbian/feminist publishing company in the world. Please request a
complete catalog. We offer personal service; we encourage and welcome direct
mail orders from individuals who have limited access to bookstores carrying
our publications.